The Cover
of Life

by R. T. Robinson

A SAMUEL FRENCH ACTING EDITION

SAMUEL
FRENCH
FOUNDED 1830
New York Hollywood London Toronto
SAMUELFRENCH.COM

ISBN   978-0-573-67010-7   Printed   in   U.S.A.   #5899

IMPORTANT BILLING AND CREDIT REQUIREMENTS

All producers of THE COVER OF LIFE *must* give credit to the Author of the Play in all programs distributed in connection with performances of the Play and in all instances in which the title of the Play appears for purposes of advertising, publicizing or otherwise exploiting the Play and/or a production. The name of the Author *must* also appear on a separate line, on which no other name appears, immediately following the title, and *must* appear in size of type not less than fifty percent the size of the title type.

THE COVER OF LIFE had its world premiere at the American Stage Company, James N. Vagias, Executive Producer; further developed at The Hartford Stage Company, Mark Lamos, Artistic Director; David Harkanson, Managing Director.

The playwright wishes to thank the following people for their support in the production of THE COVER OF LIFE: Joan Asher, Ron Cohen, Jane Factor, Andrew Goldstein, T. Harding Jones, Charles Scibetti, Theatre Production, Inc., WACT Productions, Inc., Andrew Goldstein, Bakula Productions, Inc. Albert Gates, Corey Goldstein, Michael Lintecum, Shubert Organization, Inc., Frederic Vogel, Howard Weingrow, Childs Theatrical Investments, Eric Ellenbogen, Herbert Goldsmith Productions, Inc., Thomas Henderson, Louis S. Miano, Snapshot Theatrical Productions, Inc., Edwin Wachtel, and Daniel Zitin.

THE COVER OF LIFE
had its New York premiere at The American Place Theater.

PRODUCERS:
T. Harding Jones Entertainment, Inc.
Frederic B. Vogel
Herb Goldsmith Productions, Inc.
Angels Of The Arts
Snapshot Theatrical Productions, Inc.

Wynn Handman, *Artistic Director*
Susannah Halston, *Executive Director*

Directed by Peter Masterson

CAST:
(in order of appearance)

Kate Miller	SARA BOTSFORD
Tood	ALICE HAINING
Weetsie	MELINDA EADES
Aunt Ola	CARLIN GLYNN
Sybil	KERRIANNE SPELLMAN
Addie Mae	CYNTHIA DARLOW
Tommy	DAVID SCHILIRO

SCENES

ACT I:

Scene 1	Prologue / Addie Mae Interview
Scene 2	Addie Mae and Kate / Phone
Scene 3	Dinner
Scene 4	Letter Writing
Scene 5	Mail / Phone Call To Kate
Scene 6	Tood and Tommy
Scene 7	Kate's Arrival
Scene 8	Beans
Scene 9	Confrontation
Scene 10	Sybil Letter
Scene 11	Tood and Kate / Laundry

ACT II:

Scene 12	Mer Rouge
Scene 13	Sybil's Dear John Letter
Scene 14	Photo Shoot
Scene 15	Sybil's Death
Scene 16	Pre-Funeral / Kate to Harry
Scene 17	On The Way To The Funeral
Scene 18	Kate's Good-bye
Scene 19	Tood and Tommy
Scene 20	Epilogue

CAST OF CHARACTERS

TOOD:
19 years old. Pretty, genuine, a bit of a dreamer, but determined.

SYBIL:
25 years old. Flashy. "Sophisticated" or "fast" in her crowd.

WEETSIE:
20 years old. Plain and a little plump. Very religious and very much the country girl.

AUNT OLA:
Mid-forties,but appears older. The mother-in-law of the three young women. Strong, matriarchal.

KATE:
Early/Mid-forties. Correspondent/Photographer for Life magazine. Successful woman in a man's world.

ADDIE MAE:
Mid-forties. Local newspaper reporter. Affected stylishness.

TOMMY:
20 years old. The youngest brother of the family. Eager, friendly, insecure. He is a sailor, serving in the South Pacific.

The time is September, 1943. The action of the play takes place in various locations over several weeks in Sterlington, Louisiana, a very small town.

This play is dedicated to
Ollie, Iann, John, Amy, and Linda
and is written for Rodney Edgar Armstrong.

ACT I

Scene One

(The Cliffert house is represented by a minimal set, abstract and fluid. The action of the play within the house occurs in the "living room", which contains the eating/work table, and on the "front porch". Pieces of furniture are produced as needed. Hard objects of reality, floating in space. The pieces should be that of people who have meager possessions. Prominent in the house is a large framed photograph of three young men, the Cliffert brothers, each wearing the uniform of a different branch of the military. KATE MILLER enters and addresses the audience.)

KATE. *(Holds up envelope)* Did you ever get a letter you were afraid to open? Might be good news ... might not. I've got one right here. *(Looks at letter)* It's addressed to me, Kate Miller, *Life* magazine, New York City. There's also a little heart drawn on it. Harry Luce forwarded it to me and summoning a drawl, declared *(Affecting Southern accent)* "ain't nobody supposed to open it but you." *(Lights reveal TOOD)* The letter is from Tood Cliffert ... that's right, "Tood." From Sterlington, Louisiana: 3,000 happy Christians, cornbread on every table and a pickup truck in every front yard. *(Looks at envelope again)* It's typed. Where did she learn to type? *(Pause)* I can't believe it – I'm actually afraid to open it. You see, Tood came into my life ... upper *and*

9

lowercase, a couple of years ago ... in '43. Three Southern brothers – *the Cliffert boys* – enlisted in three different branches of the military – and all on the *same day.* And their wives moved in with the boys' *mamma* for the duration of the war. It *reeked* of Americana.

(WEETSIE begins making a last minute inspection of the living room. SYBIL in a slip, holds two dresses, looking in the mirror, trying to decide. TOOD begins brushing her hair.)

KATE. *(Indicating the young women)* Three young gals in a *(Affecting Southern accent)* little bitty ol' town in Louisiana – Weetsie, Sybil and ... Tood. Harry swore to me the names alone made this Pulitzer Prize material. And the boys' mamma was named Aunt Ola. *Aunt Ola.* I could just see some little old lady up to her knees in grits.

(AUNT OLA enters, with hat on, carrying her purse, walking briskly.)

WEETSIE. Aunt Ola? Ain't you gonna stay for Addie Mae's picture? She'll be here any minute.

AUNT OLA. Decidin' between holdin' my husband's hand at the hospital or havin' my picture took by Addie Mae McGough *(Pronounced "Magoo")* – now that is a pitiful choice to start the day with.

TOOD. Aunt Ola! How is Uncle Tom?

AUNT OLA. *(Matter-of-factly)* He's alive. Accordin' to Donnette on the second floor, he's a little *too* alive for some of them nurses.

SYBIL. Bless his l'il ol', wicked heart. You give him some sugar for me, you hear?

(AUNT OLA rolls her eyes, she looks at TOOD, who smiles and waves good-bye.)

WEETSIE. *(Watching AUNT OLA leave)* Now Aunt Ola, don't you worry. It'll take more than blood poisonin' to get Uncle Tom.

AUNT OLA. *(As she leaves)* It'll take more'n poison for sure. If I thought that woulda worked I'd a tried it years ago.

(Laughs as she exits. The young women admonish her.)
(ADDIE MAE McGOUGH enters, dressed in her idea of a "working woman's ensemble." AUNT OLA notices this as she and ADDIE MAE curtly nod to each other. During the next part of KATE's speech, ADDIE MAE is greeted by the Cliffert wives and they prepare for the interview.)

KATE. The Cliffert story was first covered by local crack reporter, Addie Mae McGough for the *Sterlington Daily Enterprise.* Notwithstanding her taste in other matters, Addie Mae had a nose for news that informed her this story was bigger than Sterlington.

ADDIE MAE. Now this won't take long.

WEETSIE. Oh lord, Addie Mae, we're tickled. First an article about our husbands enlistin' together, and now an article about us. My goodness! I'm a little self-conscious about it myself, but Sybil's eatin' it up.

TOOD. Sybil thinks she's famous now. *(To SYBIL, playfully)* How can you be so famous and so poor at the same time?

SYBIL. Addie Mae, you don't mind these two, you know how country girls are.

ADDIE MAE. Well, Sybil might be onto something. I been callin' the *Times-Picayune* ever since my first Cliffert article, and when I told then that this one was gonna be on y'all, "the wives left behind," they loved it.

WEETSIE. The *Times-Picayune*?

TOOD. *(Always having to explain things to WEETSIE)* It's a *newspaper*, Weetsie. In New Orleans.

WEETSIE. *(Her own logic)* New Orleans? We ain't got no people in New Orleans.

(Shared amused look between SYBIL and TOOD.)

SYBIL. As far as Weetsie is concerned, New Orleans might as well be the moon.

KATE. Weetsie needn't have worried. *Harry* had people in New Orleans.

(KATE observes remainder of scene.)

ADDIE MAE. *(Taking notes)* Well, now, you're Sybil ... right? *(Pointedly)* I've noticed you in town.

SYBIL. I am ... *noticeable*, ain't I? Sybil Cliffert. Harrist was my maiden name. That's H-a-r-r-i-s-t. With a "t" at the end.

(Watches ADDIE MAE write it down.)

ADDIE MAE. Well ... Sybil Harrist *(Over-pronounces the "t" sound)*, everybody in northeast Louisiana is plumb fascinated by the story of the Cliffert brothers.

WEETSIE. My Jerry Don is in North Africa. North Africa! Johnny, Sybil's husband, is in Sicily. There really is a Sicily!

ADDIE MAE. Sicily! My, my!

TOOD. And Tommy is in the South Pacific.

ADDIE MAE. *(Visions of hula girls)* Oooh. Tood, wouldn't you like to go to the South Pacific?

TOOD. *(No nonsense, but not meanly)* Not while there's a war goin' on.

ADDIE MAE. You got me there! And what about Lloyd? He was too old to enlist, right?

WEETSIE. Right. Him and Lois is still here. Just up the road. He's puttin' together the Cliffert Brothers' Bait and Tackle Company for when the boys all get back.

SYBIL. Yeah, for the *brothers.*

(SYBIL and TOOD share a look of skepticism.)

ADDIE MAE. *(Catching SYBIL's and TOOD's exchanged look. Broadly, after a careful pause)* How *is* livin' together?

SYBIL. *(Pause. Lightly, but with sarcasm)* We all love it. Just love it. Don't we, Tood?

WEETSIE. It just seemed like a good idea for us all to move in with each other to save on expenses and stuff. Our allotment checks is just fifty dollars apiece, and that don't go far, especially when you're tryin' to save a little bit. And if I stayed with my people up near Crossett and Jerry Don didn't get a chance to write enough, he'd be caught between a rock and a hard place tryin' to decide whether to write to me or to his mamma. None of the boys likes to write too much.

SYBIL. I think Johnny is the only one of them that *can* actually write. You know he was in business school in Monroe when the war got in his way.

TOOD. The war is such an inconvenience for Sybil.

(TOOD and SYBIL both laugh.)

WEETSIE. Sybil thinks you ought to be able to buy Maybelline with ration stamps.

ADDIE MAE. *(Incredulously)* Well, don't they still write to each of you separately?

TOOD. Well, sometimes. If one of the boys wants to just be kinda romantic or just say something private, he'll write to us personal *(rolling her eyes at SYBIL)* and he has to put a big heart on the envelope so we all know that ain't nobody supposed to open it up.

ADDIE MAE. You mean there are times when you open each other's mail?

SYBIL. *All* the time. Unless there's a heart on it.

TOOD. It was Lloyd's idea and me and Sybil didn't get no vote. Donaldson Street ain't no democracy.

ADDIE MAE. Well, I'll be.

WEETSIE. *(Carrying on: the adult)* Well ... sharin' the letters is a good idea. Every time one of the boys writes, it's kinda like they are all writin' so we read each other's letters. And that way we hear something might near every day. Like Sybil got a letter yesterday, and Tood got one last Tuesday ... and I'll probably get one any day now.

SYBIL. Right. Jerry Don's got Weetsie so trained he don't have to draw too many of them little hearts.

WEETSIE. *(Steel)* I ain't trained, Sybil, I'm *married.* M-A-R-R-I-E-D. Look it up.

TOOD. *(Cutting SYBIL and WEETSIE off)* And it helps Aunt Ola out, to hear everything her boys writes. And we write our letters at the same time. In fact it's letter-writin' night tonight.

ADDIE MAE. My, my. Just so much to write about! *(Gathering her rather large and pretentious attaché case)* Well, I got to have this down at the paper right away, so I have

got to went. *(ADDIE MAE hands WEETSIE the framed photograph as she readies her camera)* Listen, let me get a shot of y'all holdin' this photograph of the three boys. *(They begin to pose with the photograph. ADDIE MAE observes them through her camera)* If the *Times-Picayune* has good sense, they'll put y'all's picture on the cover of the Sunday Section.

WEETSIE. *(Eagerly: Miracles do happen)* For the cover of the *Times-Picayune!* (Salutes proudly.)

TOOD. *(Amused at WEETSIE)* The *Times-Picayune!* *(Salutes in good-humor.)*

SYBIL. Aw hell, why not? *(Salutes dramatically, pushing to the center of the photo.)*

(ADDIE MAE snaps photo and exits quickly. The LIGHTS fade slowly on the three young women in their pose.)

Scene Two

(KATE reappears in LIGHT as LIGHTS fade on the three wives in their pose. Still holding the letter.)

KATE. They were too good to be true, so we'll put them on the cover of *Life*. That's what Harry thought. *(Pause)* Addie Mae's article did make it to the *Times-Picayune* which found its way to Harry's desk. He called me into his office. "Katie," he said, "I'm giving you a shot at the cover." *(Pause, flabbergasted)* The cover! The cover of *Life!* Well, I went nuts. Then the sonofabitch told me the li'l ol' pea-pickin' story. *(Total disgust)* And the reason he was sending me was because the angle was the wives – a woman's piece. A *woman's piece*. For *me*. I said, "Come on, Harry, I haven't been working the War for you, to do a piece of fluff for my first cover. He responded, "It'll be good for you." *(Pause. Reflective)* Well, Harry was right. *(Upbeat and sardonic)* He was always right. And always ... perfect. When Harry wore a white linen suit and carried the *New York Times,* he got white linen all over the *New York Times. (Pause)* Oh, let me emphasize one more time: I did not want to go. "Harry," I pleaded, "I don't even know how you get there. Trains don't go there, Harry. It's all swampland. The entire state is under water." Harry, ever the boss, said take it or leave it. I took it. So, I thought, let me get started. *(Defeated)* Correction, I thought let me get it *over with.* This was my general attitude as I made that first call. *(Gets out a notebook, looks up a number and begins as operator comes on the line)* Yes, operator, person to person to Addie Mae McGough Blackard, Sterlington, Louisiana, *(Reacts to strange phone number as she says it)* 2-7-5-9-J? *(KATE does not want to make this call)* Anything for the cover of *Life.* I had dodged bullets in Italy and taxis on Sixth Avenue, but there was no getting around Addie Mae ...

*(ADDIE MAE appears in curlers and bathrobe. There is a
    phone on a table by a chair.)*

ADDIE MAE. *(ADDIE MAE calls offstage in a loud, grating, but not mean, voice)* I've got it Sonny! *(Quick change into a genteel, businesslike tone)* Hello. This is Addie Mae McGough Blackard. *(Covers mouthpiece, loud again, shocked that she has received a person to person call)* What? *(Calls out to Sonny)* Sonny, Lou says it's person to person!

(Back to phone, annoyed at what the operator says) Yes, Lou, you know dern good and well it's me. *(Pause)* Hello?

KATE. Good afternoon.

ADDIE MAE. Afternoon? *(Nervous giggle)* It's six o'clock. Might near bedtime! You must be callin' from Mars!

KATE. *(Looks around)* Sort of. Sorry to be calling so ... late. *(Looks at her watch, not entertained.)*

ADDIE MAE. May I ask whom is calling?

KATE. *(Please! Hear the grammar?)* This is Kate Miller. Of *Life* magazine.

ADDIE MAE. *(Pause)* I'm sorry. I thought you said *Life* magazine was calling. I must have a loose connection.

KATE. No doubt. Well, this is really *Life* magazine.

ADDIE MAE. Well, this is really Addie Mae.

KATE. *(Hating this, but trying to be professional)* I am so pleased to find you.

ADDIE MAE. *(As she speaks she realizes her hair is in curlers)* Find me? Was I lost and didn't nobody tell me?! *(Nervous laughter at her own joke. She tries to continue conversation as she fixes her hair.)*

KATE. I obtained your number from the *Times-Picayune* people. Lovely article.

ADDIE MAE. Oh, my goodness, that was three months ago.

KATE. Didn't the people from the *Times-Picayune* call you and let you know that I would be contacting you?

ADDIE MAE. Well, yes, my husband said that I did get a call, but we thought somebody in town was pullin' my leg. Oh my god! *Life* magazine!

KATE. Well, Addie Mae – is it all right to call you Addie Mae?

ADDIE MAE. Honey, you can call me anything you want.

KATE. I am going to need some background on the boys.

ADDIE MAE. *(In heaven. To herself)* Background.

KATE. Your article in the *Picayune* says they are, quote, "A fine example of Southern manhood."

ADDIE MAE. No, no ... it says, "The *finest* example ..."

KATE:*(Checking the article, flatly)* So it does.

ADDIE MAE. The Clifferts helped settle this part of the country.

KATE. Did they? *(Chummier, strictly because she knows ADDIE MAE can be of help)* Addie Mae, I'm going to depend on you to give me all the help you can.

ADDIE MAE. *(Flustered)* Oh, lord. *(Then all business)* Will I get credit?

KATE. *(Amused at ADDIE MAE's assertiveness)* Yes, I'm sure we can arrange something.

ADDIE MAE. *(Blissfully)* Well, Uncle Tom was a travelin' music teacher ... goin' from church to church. That's how he met Mrs. Cliffert – Aunt Ola ... am I goin' too fast for you, Kate?

(LIGHTS fade on ADDIE MAE dictating enthusiastically to KATE. Upbeat bluegrass MUSIC plays.)

Scene Three

(AUNT OLA is setting the table. WEETSIE sits at the table, with a small note pad.)

WEETSIE. *(AUNT OLA puts down a pan of cornbread. WEETSIE quickly picks up her pencil)* Aunt Ola, what was the last thing you put in this cornbread?

AUNT OLA. About a pinch and a half of salt.

WEETSIE. A pinch and a half? Would that be about an eighth of a teaspoon?

AUNT OLA. A what?

WEETSIE. A pinch and a half. Would that be an eighth of a teaspoon?

(TOOD enters with a dish of blackeyed peas, places it on the table.)

AUNT OLA. Lord in heaven, I ain't got no idea. A pinch is a pinch.

TOOD. What are you doin', Weetsie?

WEETSIE. Writin' down all of Aunt Ola's cookin' into recipes.

AUNT OLA. *(Dryly)* She's expectin' me to die 'fore I finish supper.

WEETSIE. Aunt Ola! *(Teasing)* You so mean. Well, you know you make the best table I ever put my feet under. Includin' my own mamma's.

TOOD. *(Teasingly to AUNT OLA)* Ain't that some kinda sin, to like somebody else's cookin' better'n your own mamma's?

AUNT OLA. Yes indeed, says it right in the Bible.

WEETSIE. *(Undefeated)* Well, my mamma's is good and all, but she ain't Jerry Don's mamma.

AUNT OLA. Uh-huh. And you want Jerry Don to be able to put his feet under his mamma's table long after I'm dead and gone. Right?

WEETSIE. *(Without thinking)* Right. *(Catching herself)* When we all move up to Irvine's Lake for the Cliffert Brothers' Bait and Tackle Company, he can still have his mamma's cookin'.

AUNT OLA. Lloyd and his big ideas about startin' that fish bait farm.

TOOD. He ain't gonna have me squattin' up on Irvine's Lake, workin' for him.

WEETSIE. Tood, that ain't right. We-all agreed.

TOOD. No, *we*-all didn't. Aunt Ola, can't you see Sybil with her arms up to her elbows in a syrup bucket full of worms?

(They laugh.)

WEETSIE. Teat agreed.

TOOD. It ain't just Tommy's decision.

WEETSIE. Sure it's Tommy's decision.

AUNT OLA. Hush. Where is Sybil anyway? I told her if she wasn't here when we were ready to eat, we were gonna eat without her.

(WEETSIE, TOOD and AUNT OLA sit down at the table. SYBIL runs in carrying the mail.)

SYBIL. *(Waving allotment checks)* Surprise! Surprise! Surprise! Hey Mamma! Hey Tood!

WEETSIE. Did you wipe your feet?

SYBIL. *(Looks directly at WEETSIE and deliberately wipes feet in the middle of the living room. Smiles)* I got allotment checks! Allotment checks!

WEETSIE. They come the same day ever' month. So what's the surprise? *(Pause)* The surprise is that you actually made it into the house without cashin' yours.

SYBIL. *(Matter-of-factly)* Don't try to be funny, Weetsie. You ain't no good at it. *(Still having fun:)* And ... the new Sears and Roebuck Wish Book come!

WEETSIE. *(Firmly)* Well, you give it to me *first* this time.

SYBIL. Weetsie, you can't order a Bible from Sears and Roebuck.

(Gives her the catalogue.)

WEETSIE. Sybil, how would you know where you can order a Bible?

SYBIL. Oooh, the Bible! The Bible! I swear the stupid pissants around here don't understand nothin' that don't come out of the damn Bible. Lyin' and cheatin' and sinnin' ever' breath and then quotin' the Bible the rest of the time. *(To WEETSIE)* Don't that take an extra-lot of energy?

AUNT OLA. Are you gonna eat with us common hypocrites or not?

SYBIL. Yes, ma'am. Yes, ma'am.

AUNT OLA. I'll get another plate.

(AUNT OLA exits.)

SYBIL. Aunt Ola, you know I'm right. Weetsie, I am just being honest. Ain't that right, Tood?

TOOD. *(Amused at SYBIL)* Don't start me to lyin'.

SYBIL. That's what keeps me in trouble in this hick town.

WEETSIE. *(Almost under her breath)* Ha. That ain't what keeps you in trouble.

SYBIL. Well, for your information, Weetsie Gail Cliffert, Johnny knows everything I do. Me and him have an arrangement for while he's over yonder. We are modern.

WEETSIE. It's all right to live the way you do, but it ain't all right to die that way.

SYBIL. Christ, more Bible. *(Pause)* We are modern.
TOOD. Y'all hush. Aunt Ola's gonna hear you.

(AUNT OLA returns with a plate, cutlery and a napkin, puts it on the table. They all sit at table.)

SYBIL. I ran into Addie Mae in Bickley's Drug Store this mornin'. She was all over me like a cheap suit. Pass me that cornbread.
WEETSIE. *(To SYBIL)* Didn't you forget something?
SYBIL. *(Hasn't a clue, then with extreme politeness)* Pass the cornbread ... *please*?
WEETSIE. *(Unamused)* We got to say the blessin'.
TOOD. *(Amused, and with great relish)* And it's Sybil's turn.
AUNT OLA. Come on, Sybil. Everybody takes a turn.

(They all bow their heads.)

SYBIL. *(Solemnly, with humor)* Dear Lord ... please make us able ... to eat ever' bite on this table.
WEETSIE. Sybil!

(TOOD controls urge to laugh, AUNT OLA smiles slightly.)

AUNT OLA. I'll say the blessin'. *(Heads bow again)* Dear Lord, thank you for all you have provided. *(SYBIL and TOOD sneak an amused look at each other, then bow heads again)* Keep an eye on my boys, let 'em come home safe. *(Looks up)* And keep an eye on my girls, too. *(Bows head again.)*
WEETSIE. And Uncle Tom.

AUNT OLA. *(Without enthusiasm)* And my dear-sweet-God-fearin'-skirt-chasin'-husband, Tom. In Jesus' name we pray. Amen.

(They begin the meal.)

TOOD. *(To AUNT OLA)* How was settin' up with Uncle Tom this mornin'?

AUNT OLA. Well, the nurse on duty kept sayin' he was delirious, but I couldn't tell no difference. *(Laughs)*

WEETSIE. Well, I pray for him every night.

AUNT OLA. Don't wear yourself out.

TOOD. *(Playfully admonishing)* Aunt Ola!

AUNT OLA. *(Remembers something)* About five years ago he near 'bout did himself in *for* me. *(She begins to laugh as she tells this story)* He was polishin' that darned old pistol of his granddaddy's, and he couldn't hold it in that crippled hand. It slipped and shot off the one good finger he had. *(More laughter)* I know I ought to have been ashamed, but it tickled me to death! He always did care more about that pistol than he ever did for me.

(The others laugh and admonish her.)

TOOD. So what did Addie Mae want?

SYBIL. Oh, she was askin' how we were doin', and *(Excitedly)* what did we think about being interviewed *again.*

WEETSIE. Again? I don't see why anybody's interested in us women.

SYBIL. Well I'd love to be interviewed again. I liked being interviewed. But next time I intend to dress better and talk more.

TOOD. Why don't you just dress more and talk better instead?

SYBIL. Don't you start on me, Tood. Aunt Ola, she's startin'.

AUNT OLA. Hush. Pass me that cornbread. Oh, I got a letter from Jerry Don yesterday.

WEETSIE. *(Surprise, disappointment)* From Jerry Don? Why didn't you tell me?

AUNT OLA. There ain't nothin' to it. North Africa is different and pretty and all, but he wishes he could have some blackeyed peas and cornbread. *(Dropping subject.)*

TOOD. Just like we havin' tonight. I bet Tommy wishes he had some of this, too.

WEETSIE. What else did he say?

SYBIL. Why do you call him Tommy when everybody else calls him Teat?

WEETSIE. Did he say to say anything to me?

TOOD. Don't get smart, Sybil.

SYBIL. Don't tell me what to do.

AUNT OLA. *(Taken by surprise at WEETSIE's question, making up a response)* Uh ... yeah ... He said "Give my sweet baby a kiss" ... or something about like that.

WEETSIE. Can I read it? Where is it?

AUNT OLA. In my purse.

WEETSIE. Where's your purse?

AUNT OLA. By my bed.

(WEETSIE gets up from the table and exits.)

SYBIL. Now don't get all upset, Tood. He is called Teat 'cause he's the baby.

TOOD. He ain't no baby no more.

SYBIL. He'll always be Aunt Ola's baby. Ain't that right, Aunt Ola?

AUNT OLA. Sybil, why do you always have to stir things up?

SYBIL. To remind me I ain't dead.

AUNT OLA. I won't have it at my table.

SYBIL. *(Long pause as SYBIL begins to boil. When she reacts, it is with extreme sarcasm and irreverence)* At *your* table? I thought this was *our* table. And I thought this "castle" was home. *(Gets up from table, gets lipstick from purse. Goes to mirror and begins to put it on)* I didn't think I was a damn guest in some damn hotel. Don't forget, I did not want to move in here. Johnny made me. Don't mess with me, old woman.

TOOD. Don't talk to Aunt Ola that way!

SYBIL. Go to hell, Tood. I ain't got to take shit from either one of you.

AUNT OLA. Watch your mouth.

SYBIL. Watch my mouth? *(Looking in the mirror, humorously doing what AUNT OLA has suggested. With extreme deliberation)* Shit. *(Reveling in her irreverence)* Shit, shit, shit, shit, shit, shit.

AUNT OLA. Sybil, do you want me to spank you like you was a youngun?

TOOD. You think you so damn high and mighty.

SYBIL. *(Continuing)* Shit, shit, shit ...

(WEETSIE enters with letter.)

WEETSIE. Aunt Ola, he didn't say nothin' like that in his letter. He don't mention me in here at all. Why did you tell me he did?

AUNT OLA. He always does. He just didn't this time.

SYBIL. Little Weetsie Baby didn't get no li'l old heart again? Again?

AUNT OLA. Sybil, why do you wear hateful like you wear your mascara – too much. Now are you finished?

SYBIL. Finished with what Aunt Ola? *(Overdoing her humility)* Aunt Ola, *ma'am.* Excuse me. *Excuse me.* I don't know how to act when I'm in the *big* house. Sittin' at the *big* table. *(Sarcastic irony)* Eatin' blackeyed peas and cornbread. *(Steely)* Yes indeed, Madam Cliffert! I wonder what the poor folks is doin' tonight!

AUNT OLA. Sweetheart, you can pack your bags anytime. Ain't no law says you got to stay here.

SYBIL. Oh yes there is. Why it would just break my baby's heart if his little honey didn't stay right by the side of his dear, old, martyred mamma.

AUNT OLA. *(Furious. Clears the table)* You stay or you go. It don't matter to me. But let me tell you one thing. This is my house and this is my table and I don't give a damn if you was my own mamma, you ain't gonna act like you doin'.

(AUNT OLA exits.)

SYBIL. *(To TOOD)* Teat is such a sucker. *That's* why he's called Teat.

(LIGHTS fade slowly.)

Scene Four

(SYBIL, WEETSIE and TOOD are in different parts of the stage, writing letters to "the boys." They each hold their

*pen, thinking, looking at their mate in their mind's eye.
They think their private thoughts for some time before
they speak.)*

TOOD, SYBIL & WEETSIE. *(Gently overlapping)* Dear
Baby. I miss you. With all my heart.

SYBIL. *(Aggressively sexy)* Hey, Baby. Be sure to look
at the moon tonight. I'll look at the moon every night, just so
I know I'll be lookin' at the moon at the same time as you.

WEETSIE. Tood said she thinks she felt the baby move.
I almost started squallin, wishin' it was me. That's our first
order of business when you come home.

TOOD. I know that one of these days I'll look down this
front walk and on down Donaldson Street and I'll just see the
dust movin' under your feet. Just the dust. And I'll know. The
dust gets stirred up down there every day, but I'll know when
it's you.

SYBIL. *(Annoyed, pouty)* Oh hell, I just remembered
something. Your time is different there. What will I do if it's
always daylight there when the moon is out here?

WEETSIE. I do my best to keep Tood and Sybil off'n
each other. It just worries me and Aunt Ola sick. Blessed are
the peacemakers, that's what I always say. Me and Aunt Ola.

SYBIL. You know, every now and then I get me a little
bottle of something down at C. Domino's liquor store and I go
down to the McGough's field – Well, I sit there and look at
the moon and think of you. *(Caresses herself suggestively.)*

TOOD: I think it is a miracle that the Good Lord put us
on the Earth close enough that we could find each other. Two
people with the same hopes and dreams. We do have the same
hopes and dreams, don't we? *(Crumples up paper.)*

WEETSIE. Don't you worry Baby. Me and your sweet
mamma keeps things under control. Me and her makes a good

team. So it don't matter if you write her or me. It's all the
same. Ain't it?

SYBIL. And sometimes, Baby, I pretend you're right
there beside me and I pretend your hands are on me.

TOOD. Oh, Tommy, I have such dreams.

WEETSIE. Tood is still always hollerin' about Lloyd.

SYBIL. Hey Baby, I got a tickle right where I need you
to scratch. Ain't nobody can scratch me the way you do, Baby.

WEETSIE. The five acres right next to the landin' on
Irvine's Lake come available. Another blessin' from the Good
Lord.

SYBIL. Well, anyway, I guess I'm gonna look pretty
stupid doin' all that when the moon is up over you. What's it
gonna be here, about two o'clock in the afternoon? I can just
see old lady McGough comin' up on me in them fields, flat on
my back, squirmin' and moanin' and callin' out your name.
But I don't care. I'm gonna do it for you.

WEETSIE. Why does everybody want to change things?
I liked growin' up in my mamma's house.

SYBIL. God, I love being your woman.

WEETSIE. Tood don't know a good man when she sees
one.

SYBIL. I ain't nothin' without you.

TOOD, WEETSIE & SYBIL. God, I wish this war was
over.

WEETSIE. I wish you was home and I was in my own
house down the road from my mamma and I was sittin' in a
rockin' chair, rockin' my baby and Jerry Don, you was layin'
on the couch readin' a newspaper or Police Gazette or
something. Just plain stuff. Just ordinary. I wish it was just life
again. Just plain life. *(Overlapping with SYBIL)* Love, your
Baby.

SYBIL. *(Also overlapping)* Your sexy Baby.

(SYBIL and WEETSIE exit leaving TOOD alone on stage.)

TOOD. Dear Baby. I come out on the porch to write this. I was foldin' clothes before. I did Mrs. Holcomb's wash again. That's another seventy-five cents. Three more dollars and I can buy a bond. The clothes smelled so good cause I used lots of Clorox in the white things and they dried in the sun. They smell clean, like just bathed babies with a fresh diaper on. And they feel like a new sheet of paper – you know like from the tablets they give you at school? Not the rough tablets for usin' pencil, but the slick tablets for writing with ink. God, I loved them tablets. The slick ones. They seemed glamorous to me. Special. I thought them slick tablets could take me places I never been. I wish I had one now and it could take me to you. Not just my words, but me. Over Aunt Ola's house, past the courthouse square and on toward Texas and California. I could look down at Hollywood as I headed out over the ocean to some place I can barely dream.

(TOOD starts to dance as if she has a partner. She spins herself around etc. and as she turns one time with her arms outstretched, TOMMY appears in memory. She is swept away in a reverie, thrilling and sensuous. They both stand, looking out, remembering their last time together.)

TOMMY. Hey, look, I'm a sailor now. Bell bottoms and all. How do I look?
TOOD. *(Smiles, moving into a memory of TOMMY)* Like a hero. My hero.

TOMMY. Are you my honey?

TOOD. *(Turns, looks at him)* Always. Always your honey.

TOMMY. *(Indicating uniform)* Now don't you worry about this.

TOOD. I ain't worried. If I had my druthers, I'd had you wait just a little longer before you went in ... until after the baby gets here, but ...

TOMMY. Well, I know. But ... well, you know, with Jerry Don decidin' to enlist first and then Johnny, well, Lloyd thought it would be a good idea if we all went in together.

TOOD. *Lloyd* thought.

TOMMY. Now, don't you worry so much about Lloyd.

TOOD. What does Tommy think?

TOMMY. Come on Tood. Lloyd's gonna take care of things while we're all over there. *(No response from TOOD)* *(Overcome with his love for her)* God, I love you. Do you know Melvin McIntyre saved my life!

TOOD. *(Gentle protest, smiling)* Oh, my brother did not save your life!

TOMMY. He did, too. He said, *(Broadly)* "Hey boy, you got to come to my house and have some of my mamma's blackeyed peas and cornbread. And while you there, you might as well meet my old, ugly sister Tood."

TOOD. And he didn't say tom-turkey to me. Next thing I know I'm sittin' next to one of them good-lookin' Cliffert boys.

(They embrace, kiss.)

TOMMY. I'll build you a house from trees I cut down with my own hands. I'll make your ever' dream come true.

TOOD. Well, I got lots of them.

TOMMY. *(Confidentially)* That don't scare me.

TOOD. I'm willin' to work as hard as anybody for them too. *(Pause, looks at TOMMY)* I didn't ever think I'd meet anybody with eyes as blue as my brothers'. Did you know all my brothers got blue eyes?

TOMMY. No. But if they do, they bloodshot too ...

TOOD. Don't be mean about my brothers. They might drink a little, but they got golden hearts. Just like you. You got a golden heart, too. You're strong and funny and kind and ... gentle ... and ...

TOMMY. Shhh ... dance with me. Dance with me.

(They dance the same dance TOOD did alone earlier. Suddenly TOMMY spins off. TOOD looks out as memory fades. LIGHTS begin to dim slowly as the bluegrass MUSIC starts again, hauntingly. LIGHTS out.)

Scene Five

(WEETSIE is sewing quilt pieces together.)

WEETSIE. *(Softly, half humming, half singing)* Shall we gather at the river. The beautiful, beautiful river. *(Or similar hymn) (Looking at a piece of fabric, a young girl in love)* Oooh, Jerry Don, look at this piece. Do you remember this piece? It's from the first shirt I ever made you. This is the light blue from the dress Mamma made me when we got married. And this ...

(TOOD runs in from the porch, holding the mail. She has an almost shocked look on her face.)

WEETSIE. Tood? Are you all right? Tood! What's the matter with you?

TOOD. I got the mail.

WEETSIE. Well, the mail don't usually make you turn the color of butterbeans.

TOOD. It's registered. Mr. Buford made me sign for it before he'd give it to me.

WEETSIE. Oh my god, is it about one of the boys?

TOOD. It ain't a telegram, Weetsie, it's a registered letter. *(Pause)* From *Life* magazine.

WEETSIE. *(Tentatively, after a pause)* Do they want us to subscribe?

TOOD. Yeah, it's a personal request in a registered letter.

WEETSIE. Well open it. It ain't gonna bite you.

TOOD. All right. *(Opening letter carefully)* "September 16, 1943. Mrs. Jerry Don Cliffert ..."

WEETSIE. *(Shocked)* It's addressed to me?

TOOD. Listen. "Mrs. Thomas Cliffert, Jr., Mrs. John Cliffert. 1220 Donaldson Street, Sterlington, Louisiana. Dear Madams. *(Smiles at "madams." Has difficulty with the term "in re" which she does not recognize)* In re article published recently in the *New Orleans Times-Picayune*: The editorial staff at *Life* is considering expanding the article in an issue sometime in the near future. Additionally, our Picture Bureau wishes to discuss photographing the Cliffert family for possible consideration as a cover photograph. Please call me to coordinate my schedule in Louisiana. Further communication to follow. Signed Kate Miller, Special Correspondent."

(WEETSIE and TOOD look at each other, then back to the letter. Then WEETSIE takes it and looks at it. She reads

it silently. They look at each other again. They scream and jump up and down in excitement.)

WEETSIE. *(Suddenly stops)* Well, are you gonna call her?

TOOD. Me? I ain't ever made a long-distance call before.

WEETSIE. You got her number?

TOOD. Yeah, it's right here.

WEETSIE. Well, call her.

TOOD. Aunt Ola should call her.

WEETSIE. Aunt Ola? You should call her. You can talk. Call her.

TOOD. Well, give me a minute. *(TOOD goes to telephone and picks it up. WEETSIE stands right next to TOOD as she talks.)* Lou? It's Tood. Hey. Oh, she's fine. Uh ... Lou? *(Very nervous)* I need to ... uh ... make a call ... to New York City. Yes, that's right. Wait a minute. The number ... *(Looks at KATE's letter, is confused by the numbers)* P ... L ... 74502. *(To herself)* PL?

KATE. *(PHONE rings, KATE picks it up. All business)* Kate Miller here. *(No response from TOOD. Long pause)* Hello?

TOOD. *(Barely audible)* Hey.

KATE. Can you speak up please?

TOOD. Yes'm. *(Louder)* Hey.

KATE. *(Dryly)* Give me a hint.

TOOD. Uh ... how are you ... ma'am?

KATE. Ma'am? Who is this? Nobody calls me ma'am and gets away with it.

TOOD. *(Smiles a bit at KATE's response, then speaks with more authority)* This is Mrs. Tommy Cliffert of Sterlington, Louisiana.

KATE. Oh. *Lovely. (Very matter-of-factly)* Which one are you?

TOOD. Ma'am? *(Correcting the "ma'am")* Huh?

KATE. What's your *name*?

TOOD. Tood. Well, my real name is Ollie, but everybody calls me Tood. I don't even remember how I got the name.

KATE. Oh, Ollie. *(Thumbing through notes)* Well, in that case I know a lot about you.

TOOD. You *do*?! How come you know so much about me?

KATE. Addie Mae McGough is a veritable font of minutiae.

TOOD. Is that right? Addie Mae? *(Almost under her breath)* A font of ... minutiae. Hmmm.

KATE. Uh-huh.

TOOD. Lord, you probably know what color step-ins I wear! *(KATE doesn't understand what it means, WEETSIE is horrified)* Oh, step-ins is panties.

KATE. Oh my. Oh. How ... colorful. Well, Addie Mae is working with me on an itinerary and hotel arrangements. She's meeting me in Monroe. I'll send details.

TOOD. Hotel? There ain't no hotel here in Sterlington. There ain't even a roomin' house.

KATE. *(Covering mouthpiece)* Harry Luce, I'll strangle you.

WEETSIE. Ask her to stay with us.

TOOD. *(Covering mouthpiece)* I can't do that. *(WEETSIE urges her on, TOOD tries to be more formal)* Why don't you just stay with us?

KATE. Gosh. I don't think so. *(Covers mouthpiece)* With my bare hands.

TOOD. It ain't fancy, but it's clean.

WEETSIE. Is she gonna stay here? Oh lord, I think I'm gonna pass out.

KATE. *(Trying to be civil in unhappy circumstances)* Well, you're lovely to suggest that. We'll see.

TOOD. Well, you think about it. You'd sure be up to your knees in *colorful* then.

KATE. I'll bet. Oh, now don't count on this, but we're pulling strings to bring your husbands home for the cover. *(TOOD and WEETSIE look at each other in shock, forgetting the phone. KATE realizes what has happened)* Hello? Well ... ta.

TOOD. *(Not really hearing KATE)* Ta.

(WEETSIE and TOOD are wide-eyed as TOOD realizes KATE has hung up. TOOD hangs up the phone.)

WEETSIE. Did she say what I think she said?

TOOD. Bring the boys home. *(Complete disbelief)* They're gonna bring the boys home.

WEETSIE. *(Losing it)* Ohmigod. Ohmigod. It's a miracle. A miracle. Ohmigod. We got to tell Aunt Ola and Addie Mae. I got to call Bette Mahoney. I got to tell everybody.

TOOD. Ohmigod. I'm goin' into shock. I am. My heart feels like it's gonna fly right out of my body.

(She and WEETSIE look at each other again, scream and jump up and down again.)

WEETSIE. *(Stops jumping. Pause. Quizzically)* Ta?

(TOOD shrugs.)

(BLACKOUT)

Scene Six

(TOOD comes onto porch with laundry hamper. She looks around, thinks about TOMMY.)

TOOD. Dear Baby. There is a stillness in the house tonight because the boys are comin' home. Each of us sits in different places, different chairs, and stares into space. The boys are comin' home. The stillness is different for each of us – mine is like the air before a midsummer lightnin' storm. It is makin' me ... tremble ... with joy and achin'. The boys are comin' home.

(TOMMY enters with letter.)

TOMMY. Your letters is sure pretty soundin'.

TOOD. Why don't they let you tell me exactly where you are?

TOMMY. *(Amused)* 'Cause there's a war goin' on!

TOOD. I mean, I get out the atlas and try to figure out where you are, and all I know is the South Pacific and the South Pacific is a big place.

TOMMY. We'll make up a secret code. All right?

TOOD. All right! I'd like that!

TOMMY. Hey, you ain't gonna recognize me when I get home. I'm fillin' out so good.

TOOD. *(Laughs, touches her stomach)* Me, too!

TOMMY. Hell, now that I'm a sailor, my stupid brothers'll know I'm just as much of a man as any one of them.

TOOD. *(Registers this last comment, then to herself)* How much of a man is that? *(Eagerly, to TOMMY)* Hurry home.

*(TOOD takes shirt from hamper, dances with it. KATE enters.
She is obviously not dressed for this Southern climate.
She is carrying her camera and suitcase. She appears to
have come from another planet. She is exhausted, hot,
miserable.)*

Scene Seven

*(TOOD turns while dancing and sees KATE. TOOD is
startled.)*

KATE. Sorry, I didn't mean to startle you.

TOOD. Oh, that's all right. I was just ... daydreamin'.
Can I help you?

KATE. Oh god, please, somebody help me. *(Catches
herself, then with as much dignity as she can muster)* How do
you do, I'm Kate Miller. From *Life* magazine. *(TOOD is
immediately speechless, then, after a long pause)* Is this the
Cliffert residence?

TOOD. *(Finally, still stunned)* Yes, ma'am. *(Long pause)*
It is.

KATE. Then you are expecting me?

TOOD. *(In awe)* 'Bout like the Second Comin'.
(Remembers her appearance) Oh lord in heaven look at me. I
would have to be washin' clothes for Mrs. Holcomb when the
people from *Life* come here. *(Proudly)* She pays me.

KATE. *(As she sits, exhaustedly)* May I sit down?

TOOD. I am such a jackass. *(Catches her language)* Of
course, please sit down. Would you like to come inside?

KATE. One thing at a time. Well, how do you do? I've
just arrived in your charming little ... *(Looking around
distastefully)* hamlet.

TOOD. Uh-huh. *(Trying to be casual)* Well ... hi. I'm one of the Clifferts. The embarrassed one.

KATE. You're Tood.

TOOD. Yes'm.

KATE. Please, no "yes'm's" and "ma'am's." I don't think I could stand it.

TOOD. *(Smiles)* We talked on the telephone. Long distance.

KATE. Of course. Step-ins. *(Tight smile)* My files keep growing on you.

TOOD. Oh, you got to be kiddin'.

KATE. Addie Mae sent me as much material on this family as she could. Gospel singers turned war heroes. *Perfect.* I can tell you the people from *Life* are absolutely enthralled with this family.

TOOD. What else do you know about me? I'm not a Cliffert. Well, I *am* married to one, but that ain't been for that long.

KATE. Six months. And you are expecting a little Cliffert.

TOOD. That's right. How'd you know that? Oh, that's right – Addie Mae.

KATE. Where are the others? I've got to admit to being a little enthralled myself.

TOOD. Enthralled?

KATE. *(Explaining)* Enchanted, charmed ...

TOOD. *(Quickly, annoyed, very pointedly to KATE)* I *know* what it means. I finished tenth grade. I just ain't figured *why* you so ... enthralled.

KATE. *(Surprised, impressed with TOOD's firmness)* I apologize, Tood, I ...

TOOD. *(Humorously, but with a point)* Oh, that's all right, we get a lot of that in this here little ... hamlet.

KATE. *(Quickly, caught a bit offguard)* Oh dear, was I sounding grand? I'm sorry. I didn't mean to.

TOOD. *(They both laugh again, warming up slightly to each other)* Besides, I figure you must be pretty grand to work for *Life* magazine. Don't pay no attention to me.

KATE. Well, it's just that ... I left New York two days ago and I can't sleep on a train ... and I'm starving ... and ... hot.

TOOD. First thing you need is a big old glass of iced tea. I got iced tea so good it'll knock your papa down. *(KATE reacts. TOOD starts to go to kitchen)* Lord mercy, how did a big thing like *Life* magazine find this bunch?

KATE. *(Relaxing, becoming herself)* *Life* never sleeps.

TOOD. You take sugar in your iced tea, Mrs. Miller? Is it Mrs.?

KATE. No to sugar. No to Mrs., but you can call me, "Kate." Please.

TOOD. Well ... Kate, I just baked three of the best coconut cakes you ever flapped a lip over. I'd be honored to cut one for you. Goes real good with iced tea.

KATE. Well, O.K., just a taste. *(TOOD exits, KATE chuckles as she quickly takes out her notebook and makes a note. Amused incredulity)* Flapped a lip over.

TOOD. *(Offstage, getting cake and tea)* How long you gonna be in our little hamlet, Kate?

KATE. My assignment is to get the real scoop on the women back home, sacrificing and waiting for our boys.

TOOD. *(Entering with tea and cake)* Uh-huh. How long you 'spect that scoop's gonna take?

KATE. Dunno. You're my first impression.

TOOD. Oh lord, don't have the women back home blamin' me for nothin'. *(Laughs)* Did you decide about stayin' with us?

KATE. *(Eating some of the cake)* Well, I figured I couldn't pass up the opportunity to really get to know everyone. And I don't think I could take long stretches of Addie Mae.

TOOD. *(Light laugh)* She's a piece of work, ain't she? *(Catching herself)* Oh, she's nice and all, and she does a lot of good for people and stuff.

KATE. *(Smiles)* I know what you mean.

TOOD. Aunt Ola thinks she's too uppity and talks too much. One time she said if Addie Mae didn't shut up, she was gonna split her tongue and run her leg through it. *(There is a moment of absolute silence as the statement sinks in to KATE. Then a shared laugh)* There I go being colorful again.

(WEETSIE enters, obviously angry. She doesn't see KATE. Through the following scene, TOOD tries to regain control. WEETSIE and SYBIL overlap each other's dialogue.)

WEETSIE. Tood, why can't you let well enough alone? I just come from Lloyd and what he told me was bad enough, but then I go into Bickley's Drug Store to pick up a prescription for Mamma. And there is Sybil, puttin' on lipstick from one of the displays – and I ain't talkin' no free-sample either. And Mr. Bickley is havin' a hissy fit, and Sybil is tellin' him it's good advertisement for the store. That, on top of you ...

TOOD. *(Trying to "cover")* What is the matter with you, Weetsie?

WEETSIE. Why in Jesus' sweet name are you sendin' Teat all this mess about movin'?

(SYBIL bursts in, not seeing KATE.)

SYBIL. Weetsie Cliffert, I thought Tood was the ignorant hick around here. But *you* – *(To TOOD)* She was *screamin'* at me in the middle of Bickley's Drug Store.

TOOD. *(Humiliated. KATE is amused by it all)* Weetsie, Sybil, don't do this.

SYBIL. Screamin'. Like a stuck hog.

WEETSIE. *(To SYBIL)* You're pitiful.

SYBIL. A big ol' *fat* stuck hog.

WEETSIE. *(Back to TOOD)* Ain't you ever heard of family, Tood? This is a good one. Why you got to mess it up.

SYBIL. *(To TOOD)* It's all perfectly logical. Old man Bickley don't let you sample nothin' before you buy it. *(Back to WEETSIE)* What happens if you get the wrong shade? You know I can't *eat* lipstick. You want a reason to get in a moral outrage ... *(SYBIL sees KATE and after a moment senses who she is. WEETSIE turns to see KATE)* Oh shit. *(To KATE)* Hey. I promise I didn't get this red face at Bickley's Drug Store. *(Extends hand to KATE, trying to make a good impression)* I'm Sybil.

KATE. How do you do? I'm Kate Miller. *(Pause)* From *Life* magazine.

(WEETSIE is humiliated, and faints.)

(BLACKOUT)

Scene Eight

(AUNT OLA is sitting on the porch, snapping beans. KATE enters, carrying her camera.)

AUNT OLA. *(Observing KATE)* Addie Mae takin' you on another whirlwind tour of North Louisiana?

KATE. Yes. Today it's crayfish and palmetto fans. *(AUNT OLA smiles)* Whatever did you put in that iced tea last night? It must have been drugged for me to sleep like that.

AUNT OLA. It's that old attic fan, just lulls you right out.

KATE. *(Observes AUNT OLA for a moment and then picks up snapped bean)* All these years I thought they grew that way.

AUNT OLA. *(Chuckles)* Uh-huh. And you the big, smart reporter for *Life* magazine?

KATE. Well, come on, Aunt Ola, give me a break. The only thing I use my kitchen for is to water my plants.

AUNT OLA. *(Chuckles. Pause, amazed)* You live by yourself in New York City?

KATE. *(Amused)* I do.

AUNT OLA. Lord, I can't even imagine that.

KATE. You might surprise yourself.

AUNT OLA. Oh lord, I ain't got the heart for any more surprises in my life. Kate, are my boys really on their way home?

KATE. Yep. There's some delay with Johnny, but he'll make it.

AUNT OLA. Just like that.

KATE. Just like that. Are you excited about seeing your boys?

AUNT OLA. They'll get to see their daddy alive. I'm excited about that.

KATE. Oh, I'm sorry, Aunt Ola. I didn't realize ... What will you do?

AUNT OLA. Same old, same old. Ain't much choice about that.

ADDIE MAE. Yoo-hoo!

AUNT OLA. *(Laughs, enjoying KATE)* Well, don't let Addie Mae wear you out. Poor old Sonny ain't breathed a relaxin' breath since the day they got married.

(ADDIE MAE enters, approaches porch.)

ADDIE MAE. *(Admiring KATE)* My goodness, you are just a glory this mornin'! A mornin' glory! Ain't that right, Aunt Ola?

AUNT OLA. Well, I was tellin' her the very same thing when you walked up.

ADDIE MAE. Well, I'd love to sit around and talk all mornin' *(AUNT OLA looks mischievously at KATE)* but, lord, I got a list of things to show Kate as long as my arm. *(To KATE)* You know you said you wanted background, and background you gonna get! Come on! *(Starts to leave, notices KATE is not right behind her, turns, and with more authority)* Come on!

KATE. *(Smiling)* O.K., let's go. *(TOOD comes out of the house)* Tood, I'll be back later.

(AUNT OLA goes back to snapping beans. TOOD watches where KATE has gone. After a moment:)

TOOD. She's something ain't she. *(AUNT OLA smiles, looks at TOOD, who is pensive, looking away)* Aunt Ola?

AUNT OLA. *(Knowing something is on TOOD's mind)* Here grab some of these beans.

(TOOD takes some beans in her apron and starts snapping them. Quiet.)

TOOD. How is Uncle Tom?

AUNT OLA. Well, Dr. Pollard said he ain't pinched a nurse in three days, so I figure he must be about dead. *(They laugh at this)* What absolutely amazes me is that one of them nurses ain't pulled the plug on that old fart. *(More laughter)*

Some women just don't seem to mind. *(Pause)* How you doin', Baby?

TOOD. All right.

AUNT OLA. Did you really say "Aunt Ola" cause you wanted to know how Tom was doin'?

TOOD. Well ... *(Finally gathering her courage)* Aunt Ola? Why are your sons all like they are? Except for Tommy? He ain't like the rest of them.

AUNT OLA. As far as Tommy is concerned, he needs a little more of them, if you ask me.

TOOD. What part of them do you wish on him?

AUNT OLA. Tommy ought to be a little tougher. If he was tougher he would stand up to them. *(Pointedly)* If he was tougher he would take his beautiful new wife and baby and leave this town when he gets back.

TOOD. That's why I said "Aunt Ola."

AUNT OLA. I know that.

TOOD. You wouldn't be real hurt if we moved someplace? Not too far, but just far enough to ...

AUNT OLA. Lord no, I wouldn't mind. I ain't dead, you know. I'd love to go visit my younguns in Dallas or Atlanta or someplace like that.

TOOD. Oh Aunt Ola, is it wrong to want me and Tommy to have a world of our own?

AUNT OLA. Come here. *(AUNT OLA takes her hands)* I know my boys is all stuck on themselves and hard on the people that loves 'em. Poor old Sybil, she ain't got no idea yet what a real dog Johnny's gonna be. And if Lois lives to see her grandkids, it will surprise me. But there she is. *(Pause)* The boys come by it natural.

TOOD. Uncle Tom? He don't seem so bad.

AUNT OLA. He ain't so bad. Now. *(Smiles at TOOD, amused by the coming story)* He changed, because he had a *(Grandly)* religious experience.

TOOD. *(Awe)* He did?

AUNT OLA. *(Solemnly)* He seen a cross. *(Punchline)* Burnin' in his front yard!

TOOD. *(Flabbergasted)* The Klan?!

AUNT OLA. Yeah, the Klan! They didn't just go after colored folks and the white folks that helped 'em. They thought they was God's Little Army and if a good Christian white man started back-slidin' ... well, they provided him a little help to get back on God's Highway.

TOOD. My lord, what did he do?

AUNT OLA. Well, I was big pregnant with Teat.

TOOD. Aunt Ola, please don't call him Teat.

AUNT OLA. I called him Teat for twenty years.

TOOD. Yes ma'am. *(Smiles)*

AUNT OLA. I was pregnant with ... Tommy. *(TOOD smiles)* And me and the younguns had wore our tails out makin' that stringy crop of beans. But then about September, Tom starts helpin' out. Gettin' the crop in. And we do get it in. And Tom takes it to town to sell. He left on a Monday and he didn't come back for two weeks. *(Pause)* He sold them crops and checked into the Louisiana Hotel in Monroe – with some doe-eyed heifer. Oh yeah, had himself a high old time. And he didn't have a cent when he come home. Three younguns – one in diapers! One on the way! And not a cent. And nothin' in the fields to eat. *(Looks at TOOD)* Oh yeah, they come by it natural.

TOOD. What did you do?

AUNT OLA. *(Suddenly realizing – seemingly for the first time. Amazed at the fact)* Nothin'. I didn't do nothin'.

TOOD. Why do we fall in love with them?

AUNT OLA. *(Starts to move inside)* What difference does that make? We do. *(Turns back)* They got this ... I don't know ... "gift", I reckon. You know they all good-lookin'.

Tom Cliffert was the purtiest thing I'd ever seen *(Momentary love)* ridin' a horse up to my daddy's church, singin' loud as he could. *(Back to reality)* And they can be so sweet, sugar wouldn't melt in their mouths. And I see it happen to every one of you girls. My boys come on like they are gentlemen, and they got such dreams and they gonna burn up the world and make all your dreams come true. They gonna rescue you. Just like Tom was gonna rescue me. They sweep you off your feet. And compared with the rest of these pitiful, old, slobberin' red-neck share-croppers, my boys look pretty good. *(Pause)* It's just after they get you.

(AUNT OLA goes inside. TOOD looks out. LIGHTS fade.)

Scene Nine

(WEETSIE and AUNT OLA are crocheting. AUNT OLA half-heartedly teaches WEETSIE. KATE enters in her robe. It is late in the morning and she is just getting up. She stumbles in with coffee.)

WEETSIE. Well, good afternoon.
KATE. Oh my god, is it afternoon?
WEETSIE. Not quite. Just pickin' at you. *(SYBIL enters with a letter, which she seals. She is wearing a new dress that Aunt Ola has made for the* Life *article)* Why it won't be afternoon for another half-hour or so.
AUNT OLA. Mind your own business, Weetsie.

(KATE nods absent-mindedly to SYBIL as she picks up phone receiver.)

SYBIL. *(Kisses envelope, leaving imprint)* Over there, over there, think of me, think of me in my underwear! *(Laughs)* Did you hear that one Kate?

WEETSIE. *(Looking at SYBIL's outfit)* Why are you *wearin'* that? You know that is for the cover of *Life*. Aunt Ola?!

AUNT OLA. Mind your own business, Weetsie.

KATE. *(Into phone)* Hi, Lou! Yep, it's Kate from New York again. Yep. Same call as the others.

AUNT OLA. Ask Lou how her mamma is doin'.

KATE. *(Very uncomfortable at this)* Uh ... Lou, Aunt Ola wants to know how your mamma is doing. *(To AUNT OLA)* Fine. They still don't know what that thing on her elbow is. *(Back to phone)* Oh, thanks, Lou.

SYBIL. What you makin', Aunt Ola?

AUNT OLA. A mess. I keep losin' count. *(Looks at WEETSIE.)*

KATE. Hi, Harry! What? Honey, you gotta speak up. It's so humid down here, the sound waves stick together.

(Laughs at her own joke, continues conversation silently.)

SYBIL. I reckon *you* makin' the *same mess* as Aunt Ola, right?

WEETSIE. No. I'm makin' a baby blanket.

SYBIL. You can't wait to start churnin' out them babies, can you Weetsie? *(WEETSIE ignores SYBIL, who suddenly seems isolated)* Hey Kate, come go to town with me. I'll take you to the Blue Front. New York ain't got nothin' on the Blue Front Cafe.

KATE. *(Smiles, shakes head "no" to SYBIL)* Well, Harry, actually the first few days have been ... fun. Lotsa sitting around the porch. Lotsa girl talk.

(TOOD enters with an envelope and letter. SYBIL moves to her.)

SYBIL. Hey, Tood. Come go with me. I got a little party in my purse. *(Pulls out a small liquor bottle.)*

TOOD. *(She is hurt and angered by the letter)* Huh? *(Still distracted by the letter)* Uh. I'm sorry Sybil ... uh ... maybe I'll catch up with you later.

SYBIL. Oh, Tood, ain't nobody around here can catch up with me. *(Laughs as she exits)* Bye! I'm off like a dirty shirt!

KATE. Well, I'm just about finished here. So, I think you can go ahead with the article. I'll just wait till the boys get here, and take the cover shot. They should start arriving right away. *(Laughs at something HARRY says, all turn to look at her)* Harry wants to know if all the houses here are built on stilts to protect people from alligators. *(Laughs. No response from the others. KATE tries to save the moment, dismissing HARRY's ignorance)* Yankees. *(Back to phone)* Yes, right, I change trains in Atlanta. I'll call you before I leave.

WEETSIE. *(Tentatively)* Tood? Can't you say hi?

TOOD. *(Flatly)* Hi.

KATE. Ooh! Is that a letter from Tommy?

TOOD. *(Firmly)* It's got a heart on it. It's private.

WEETSIE. Ooh! A love letter!

TOOD. *(Unmoved)* Yeah, a love letter. Now I got a love letter for you Weetsie. If I hear of you writin' Tommy again, I will pull every hair out of that blonde head.

WEETSIE. *(A bit scared)* Tood, we got company.

TOOD. Miss Weetsie Gail here wrote Tommy I was gonna ruin this family. *(WEETSIE starts to move off)* Get your butt back here. Me, ruin this family, when I am tryin' to save Tommy's family. *(Touching stomach)* We are Tommy's family now.

(WEETSIE erupts.)

WEETSIE. You are gonna ruin this family. We *need* y'all's money. Lloyd has got to make a down payment before long and we *need* that money. Jerry Don don't want nothing to happen to the fish bait farm. And I want what Jerry Don wants. And you're gonna mess it all up.

(TOOD goes inside and KATE goes after her.)

AUNT OLA. Weetsie, you and Lloyd ought to be ashamed of yourselves. Don't you know things change.
WEETSIE. Not if you don't let 'em. *(PHONE rings. WEETSIE goes in to answer it)* Hello. What? Uh ... no. No, there ain't no man here. Oh. Well ... just a minute. *(To AUNT OLA)* He says he needs to talk to a man ... because it's important.

(AUNT OLA takes phone from WEETSIE, and begins in a syrupy-sweet stream which turns angry.)

AUNT OLA. This is Ola Cliffert. I hate to disappoint you, but there ain't no man here. Ain't nothin' here but a bunch of old, fat, pitiful, squallin' women. And it's a miracle that we have managed to stay alive, ain't it? And one more thing, mister, I want you to kiss my old, fat, pitiful, squallin' behind. *(She hangs up with a bang.)*

(BLACKOUT)

Scene Ten

(SYBIL is sitting on the grass in the McGoughs' field. She has a bottle of bourbon and a champagne glass. She takes out a picture of JOHNNY.)

SYBIL. Hey, Baby. *(Modeling sundress)* See this? Your mamma made it for the picture. For the cover of *Life* magazine! It's got a jacket to it, but when I wear the jacket, you can't see my titties. I wanted you to see my titties. *(Pours drink. Languidly, pondering)* Let me see. This drink is to the day I met you. *(Drinks it down, like a shot)* The first day of my life. You walked across that old wood floor at the Bayou Room Lounge and just come right up to me and said – you remember what you said? I do. I remember every word you ever said to me. You said, "Well, if you ain't the most woman I ever laid eyes on." You did. And right at that moment I knew it was true. And since then I poured my heart and soul into being the most woman you ever laid eyes on. *(Pours another drink)* This one is to the way you throw your head back and squeal when I let my slip shimmy down my legs. *(Laughs, then suddenly quiet and desperate)* Oh, Johnny. I'm so lonesome. *(Lightens up, smiles)* I wish my head was layin' in the small of your back. I am goin' crazy for some kind of life around here. I go down to the Blue Front just to keep my sanity. And believe me, people talk. *(To herself)* People talk. But we ain't like the rest of 'em, right Baby? We are modern. And this one *(Poises as if to pour another drink)* is because I want to get drunk. *(Swigs from bottle instead)* 'Cause I can't stand it any more without you.

(Begins to dance slowly as LIGHTS fade.)

Scene Eleven

(TOOD is at washtub, washing clothes. KATE has a glass of iced tea.)

KATE. Mmmmm. This tea is so good it would knock down my father. *(TOOD smiles at KATE)* Aunt Ola said you have taken in more wash. Don't you get tired of so much laundry?

TOOD. If I thought it would help me and Tommy to get outta here, I'd keep this whole town in clean clothes. Besides, I ain't got no choice. In Monroe they started hirin' women at the paper mill, but I ain't in Monroe. Women in Monroe got a chance. Anyways, I might near got my first hundred dollars.

KATE. My goodness. I'm impressed.

TOOD. Don't be. Hard work is the easy part.

KATE. Is it that important? To get out of here?

TOOD. It ain't gettin' out of *here* so much. It's just ...

KATE. It's just ... what?

TOOD. *(Smiles)* Is everything I say gonna wind up in *Life* magazine?

KATE. 'Course not. But, Tood, I am a reporter. I see things.

TOOD. You know, Kate, the day me and Tommy got married at my mamma's house, I was happy as a dead pig in the sunshine.

KATE. Aren't you still?

TOOD. Well, now I can see that as soon as Tommy comes back here and we settle down – right here on Donaldson Street – it ain't gonna be just our life. The rest of them will be raisin' our younguns, countin' our money, *(Meaningfully)* makin' our bed. *(Pause)* You got any New York advice?

KATE. God no, not about men. I always felt as soon as I got close to a man, I started to shrink. And if I ever said "I do", I'd disappear.

TOOD. Don't you ever need a man? Want a man?

KATE. Two separate things. I suppose I get as much as I want.

TOOD. I see.

(PHONE rings inside. WEETSIE answers phone silently.)

KATE. Besides you don't get any points for being independent. You get sweet little things like "spinster", "old maid", and worse.

TOOD. Yeah, but you have a say in what you do.

KATE. Yeah, me, Harry Luce, and my mother. *(Laughs)*

(WEETSIE comes to the door.)

WEETSIE. It's for you, Mrs. Miller.

KATE. Oh, thanks. By the way, why don't you call me "Kate"?

WEETSIE. Oh, I don't think I could do that. My mamma would shoot me if she knew I called an older woman by her first name.

(She goes back inside.)

KATE. *(To TOOD)* Well, on that note.

(They both laugh.)

(KATE goes to phone, speaks silently. The lights on the house are dim. It has turned to dusk. TOOD "writes" a letter to TOMMY. Lights come up on TOMMY reading it.)

TOOD. *(Long pause)* Dear Tommy. I was talkin' to the woman from *Life* today. She sure can ask the questions. And I answer every one of them as honestly as I can. Oh, Tommy, she's so ... unusual. Funny. She's a good listener. She wanted to know all about my family before I was a Cliffert. She actually wants to know about me.

TOMMY. *(Matter-of-factly)* Tood, do you love me? Really love me?

TOOD. So I was tellin' her about my brothers and my daddy. You know, that I don't remember too much about him. I wonder if I have any of him in me? And how much of him do my brothers have. They was all so little when he died, and they grew up without a daddy, and I wonder what that has to do with their drinkin' and all. I told Kate I thought they must be *incomplete* ... somehow. *(Pause)* Oh, Tommy, all my letters to you is so easy soundin' ...

TOMMY. Your letters have all started soundin' crazy to me.

TOOD. ... and I don't want this letter to upset you ...

TOMMY. They scare me.

TOOD. ... because ... it might not be so easy.

TOMMY. They make me think you don't believe in me.

TOOD. But, I think I am finally sendin' you a love letter. A real love letter. About real love. And it frightens me.

TOMMY. What would I do without you, Tood? I try. I try to be what you want. You always say I got so much of Mamma in me. And I'm afraid I got too much.

TOOD. Oh, Tommy, I don't want this baby here inside of me to be incomplete. It'll be half of both of us, right? And I don't mean our blood and stuff. I mean our souls.

TOMMY. It ain't easy bein' the baby. With nothin' but older brothers callin' you Teat. Like you was a runt.

(Pleading, almost in tears) As long as I can remember, I wanted to not be Teat.

TOOD. I look at that empty field next to your mamma's house, knowin' that you dream of buildin' a house right there. *Right next door.* And sometimes I get so mad at that half-acre, I could scream. I even throw rocks at it sometimes! Is that why my knuckles is raw from washin' other people's underwear – to build *that* house? Or for the damned Cliffert Brothers' Bait and Tackle Company? *Lloyd's* Bait and Tackle Company – that's what it'll be *and you know it.*

TOMMY. The bait and tackle company is my chance to be a man in this family! Tood, what is wrong with wantin' that? What's wrong with my kind of dreamin'?

(LIGHTS fade on TOMMY.)

TOOD. *(Screaming in anguish)* I DON'T WANT TO DIG WORMS FOR LLOYD WHEN YOU COME HOME! *(Broken, frightened)* All I want is *a say.* In my own life. What is wrong with my kind of dreamin'?

(LIGHTS fade on TOOD.)

END OF ACT ONE

ACT II

Scene Twelve

(The top of Red Hill, on the outskirts of Sterlington. TOOD is discovered. She is sitting alone, looking out. KATE enters, carrying a picnic basket.)

TOOD. Hey. You found it.

KATE. Addie Mae found it. I got into the car and said. "The lookout on Red Hill and step on it." Just like a cab in New York. Between the two of you, I've seen a whole lot of North Louisiana in the last couple of weeks. *(Pause, looking at the terrain)* So. Here I am. Red Hill.

TOOD. They call it Red Hill 'cause there ain't nothin' around here for miles except red clay.

KATE. Oh, it's pretty up here. I didn't realize you had hills this high.

TOOD. This is the highest point in Morehouse Parish. You can see almost all the way to Mer Rouge. *(Pronounced: ma ROOJ.)*

KATE. Mer Rouge? *(Realizes it is French)* As in *(With a French accent)* mer rouge? Meaning the Red Sea? From the Bible? *(Looks out)* Wouldn't you know.

TOOD. Is *that* what it means? Huh. All this time it was just Mer Rouge to me. I knew it meant something, but ... Huh. That's pitiful, ain't it? I been comin' up here since I was a youngun and I didn't even know where I was. The Red Sea. *(Looks out in amazement.)*

55

KATE. I'm just full of worthless information, aren't I? I'll get more profound as the day goes on. It's just a little early for me.

TOOD. Oh, that's right. You city folks sleep all day and play all night.

KATE. Right. I'll get going in a minute. Addie Mae packed a breakfast picnic. We could be up here for weeks and never go hungry. Want some coffee?

(TOOD nods yes. KATE takes out thermos and two cups, pours as TOOD looks out at the Red Sea.)

TOOD. *(Triumphantly)* I been up since 5:30.

KATE. *(Mock shock)* AM?

TOOD. *(Smiles)* Yes. AM. You know us country people. Why, by 6:30 I done milked five cows and baled hay and canned a bushel of peaches.

KATE. You *are* joking?

TOOD. *(Laughing)* Uh-huh. *(Dryly)* We ain't got no cows.

KATE. I see.

TOOD. Or hay or peaches for that matter.

KATE. Well, here you are – the best apple turnovers that Addie Mae's mamma could bake. Very tasty.

TOOD. *(Playfully formal)* Why, thank you. *(Takes a bite, sips coffee)* I love it up here. 'Specially when it's early and still cool.

(They sit, eat, silence. Finally, TOOD speaks. A deeply earnest inquiry.)

TOOD. What is it like ... in New York City?

KATE. *(Off-handedly)* Just like the movies. You go to movies, don't you?

TOOD. Well, I been a few times. Mostly on Saturday and all they showed was serials and they was all for boys – Flash Gordon and stuff. The girls went 'cause the boys went.

KATE. There, you see? Just like New York. *(Laughs)* Didn't you ever see *any* movies about New York?

TOOD. Yeah. A few.

KATE. Well, then you describe New York to me.

TOOD. *(Likes the idea, thinks)* Big.

KATE. Yes.

TOOD. Noisy.

KATE. Well, not to me.

TOOD. With all that traffic and stuff?

KATE. It's funny, it sounds like the ocean to me. Kind of a gentle roar. And believe me, nothing in Manhattan is as loud as a goddamn cricket in your bedroom at three o'clock in the morning,

TOOD. *(Laughs)* Fast. Exciting. I figure you wake up ever' mornin' tremblin', wonderin' what's gonna happen that day.

KATE. Yes. But that's not always so good.

TOOD. Expensive.

KATE. I suppose.

TOOD. And the women all have jobs.

KATE. What movies have you seen? *(Laughs)*

TOOD. *(Long pause, another deeply earnest inquiry)* What are the *men* like?

KATE. Well ...

TOOD. Are they different from men down here?

KATE. *(Pondering, searching)* Well, you know, I work almost exclusively with men. And they're great.

TOOD. Mr. Luce? What's he like?

KATE. Harry? Oh, Harry's my buddy. Great. Good boss. Attentive. He's a great guy. Great.

TOOD. What makes him so great?

KATE. He treats me like one of the boys.

TOOD. And that's great?

KATE. *(Surprised. She has never considered the question before)* Why ... why, yes. *(A bit uncertain)* Of course. Very great. It keeps me from editing recipes for *Good Housekeeping.*

TOOD. *(Long pause)* Do the men up North pay any attention to the women?

KATE. *(Again surprised by the question)* How do you mean, Tood?

TOOD. Well ... *(Smiles)* Seems like around here as soon as you are born, they take a look at your privates. *(KATE is surprised and amused at TOOD's openness)* It's like – you're gonna think I'm awful – it's like – they can *see* a man ... you know his ... thing. It's just right there. And everybody pays attention. But a woman. Her stuff is all inside and you can't see it and instead of figurin' out that it's all inside, people just figure they ain't got nothin'.

KATE. Where did you learn all this?

TOOD. Everybody knows this stuff.

KATE. Everybody doesn't. Believe me.

TOOD. Women do – after a while. But they keep it secret. Like they think they're being mysterious or something.

KATE. You're so goddamn right. Tood, do the women around here talk about this?

TOOD. No. They just get nervous and change the subject to younguns or cookin' and stuff. Oh, they pretend to stick together and all, but they don't. I'm always wonderin' why women don't stick together. It's like they're afraid of something.

KATE. Tood?

TOOD. Yes'm? *(TOOD realizes her mistake)* What?

KATE. Why did you want me to meet you here this morning?

TOOD. So you could help me see farther from up here than I can by myself.

KATE. *(Very moved and impressed by the conversation)* Tood, you *see* fine. I *should* be taking notes.

TOOD. *(Long pause)* Kate, I feel like you're becomin' my friend. I don't think I ever had a real friend before. Kinda like an older sister or something. And I ain't never had nothin' but brothers. And you come in here like something from outerspace, and then poof, you'll be gone. And why you? It don't make no sense.

KATE. I feel it too, Tood, and it makes sense to me. At least it's beginning to. Maybe I should give Harry Luce more credit. *(To herself)* A woman's piece.

TOOD. Huh?

KATE. Nothing. Private joke.

TOOD. I'm scared. When Tommy comes home for the picture, we got to face things. He is gonna have to choose. And I know what's gonna happen. It's like I can see a tornado on the horizon just over yonder, and I know it's headin' right this way and I'm scared that afterwards there ain't gonna be nothin' standin'.

KATE. You don't know that, Tood.

TOOD. Like you said, Kate, I *see* fine.

KATE. And what do you see right now, Tood?

TOOD. A sea. A great big red sea. That's what I see right now.

KATE. *(Grandly, trying to lighten the moment)* The mer rouge!

TOOD. *(Suddenly overcome with sobs)* And I'm drownin' in it.

(TOOD puts her head on KATE's shoulder and cries. KATE doesn't quite know what to do, but she's deeply moved. She just holds TOOD tightly as the LIGHTS fade.)

Scene Thirteen

(It is late the same evening. The evening meal is long over. Everybody has gone to bed. TOOD is sitting on the porch. WEETSIE comes to the porch door.)

WEETSIE. Tood? Why don't you go to bed? What you doin' out here anyway?

TOOD. Waitin' up for Sybil.

WEETSIE. For what? An update on all the celebrities down at the Blue Front?

TOOD. *(Cautiously)* A letter came today. From Johnny. And I opened it.

WEETSIE. *(Surprised, amused)* You opened it?

TOOD. *(Embarrassed)* Well, there wasn't no heart on it ... and I ...

WEETSIE. Well, where is it? I want to read it.

TOOD. *(Meaningfully)* No you don't.

(There is a long silence. WEETSIE and TOOD look at each other, WEETSIE realizes what TOOD means.)

WEETSIE. Oh my lord, is it another woman?

TOOD. Yeah! And he didn't even put a heart on it!

WEETSIE. *(Another long pause, WEETSIE doesn't know what to say)* I knew he was gonna do something stupid like that. If that don't beat all.

TOOD. I knew I shouldn't have opened it. I knew it. Anyway, I stayed up to be with her when she reads it.

(SYBIL is heard OFFSTAGE.)

SYBIL. *(Singing)*
What a dance do they do,
Lordy how I'm missin' you.
Hey – hey, Uncle Judd,
It's so sweet to beat your feet
In the Mississippi mud.

WEETSIE. Here she comes. Well, I reckon I'll stay too.

TOOD. No Weetsie, you go on to bed. I'll talk to her.

WEETSIE. But this is a family matter ...

TOOD. No it ain't. It's a Sybil and Johnny matter. Now go on.

WEETSIE. *(As she leaves)* I don't know who died and made you queen around here.

(WEETSIE exits, but stays just out of sight. SYBIL enters. She is drunk. She is dancing around, laughing, stumbling.)

TOOD. *(Tentatively)* Sybil?

SYBIL. *(Startled)* Who's that? Tood? I thought all good little girls was in bed by nine o'clock.

TOOD. Sybil? You drunk?

SYBIL. No. I am not drunk. *(Grandly)* I am *intoxicated.* Besides, it ain't none of your business, Tood.

TOOD. I didn't stay up this late to fight with you, Sybil.

SYBIL. Who's fightin'? I'm in too good a mood to fight.

TOOD. Why you in such a good mood?

SYBIL. C. *(Pause)* C. Domino. I'm in a good mood because of C. Domino. C stands for Cataldo, but everybody call him C.

TOOD. I know C. Domino.

SYBIL. Yeah, I know you do. C's got a whole section of cheap wine he calls the McIntyre Wall. *(Laughs)*

TOOD. Why are you in such a good mood because of C?

SYBIL. Just let me say that Italians know how to move. And I can just hear your little mind goin' now. What's she mean by that? What she doin' with C. Domino? Well, I ain't gonna worry about you. Not tonight. I ain't gonna live on dreams like you Tood. Dreams is stupid. When this damn war is over you'll see which of us makes it in this world. You got dreams and I got Johnny. And me and him got everything it takes and we are gonna make it big. We are modern. So you just hide and watch.

TOOD. Honey, don't you ever worry about Johnny? You know what you're doin' ain't right.

SYBIL. Oh God, don't preach to me.

TOOD. What if something happens?

SYBIL. Like what?

TOOD. Like gettin' pregnant?

SYBIL. Now, just a damn minute. I said C. Domino could dance. I didn't say nothin' else. Besides, everybody don't have to worry, poor little Sybil can't get pregnant. *(Straightforwardly, almost triumphantly)* I got *female* problems!

(SYBIL looks at TOOD defiantly, daring her to say anything

Maybe man wanted child?

about what she has just revealed. TOOD, understanding this, still tries to express concern, cautiously.)

TOOD. Oh, Sybil ... I'm sorry ... I ... didn't know ...

(TOOD stops speaking, not knowing what to say. TOOD is deeply affected by SYBIL's admission, and wants to reach out to her. SYBIL will have none of it.)

SYBIL. *(Not letting TOOD get melancholy)* Well, don't start squallin'. *(Matter-of-factly)* The last thing a woman needs is a youngun.

TOOD. *(Still trying to help)* Does Johnny know?

SYBIL. *("Up" again)* Of course he knows. That's one of the reasons he's so crazy about me. We can fool around all we want and no worries about younguns. We are modern.

TOOD. I see. Sybil, what if ... being modern ... don't work out like you got it planned? What then?

SYBIL. *(Smugly)* You got to have confidence. *(Suddenly focusing)* What are y'all doin'? Spying? If I don't show up for supper, do y'all sit around and wonder who old Sybil is up to tonight? This entire bunch makes me sick.

TOOD. *(Imperturbable)* Fine. Fine. Here. This came today. I read it because it wasn't marked personal.

SYBIL. *(Snatching the letter, opening it as she speaks)* You what?! I have told you all that I don't go along with that crap about letters. What is addressed to me is mine!

TOOD. Well, anyway, I opened it. And I stayed up in case you needed anybody.

SYBIL. *(Suddenly frightened)* What's the matter? Is he hurt?

TOOD. No, he ain't hurt. I'm going to bed. You've made it clear you don't need anybody in this bunch.

(TOOD starts to leave but hangs back.)

SYBIL. *(Reading)* Dear Baby, I hope this finds you O.K. *(SYBIL sees TOOD hasn't gone, says firmly)* Goodnight. *(TOOD starts to leave again as SYBIL turns around to continue letter. TOOD hangs back)* It is a mess over here, but really not so bad. I'm just tired a lot. Anyway, I guess I ought to get right to the point. You know I love you, Baby, and I always will ...

(SYBIL continues to read silently. She is broken, lost. TOOD approaches her and SYBIL straightens up immediately.)

SYBIL. *(Stoically, with bemusement)* Hell, this woman ain't even Italian. I might could have understood that. Johnny put a bullet through my heart with a woman from Memphis, Tennessee.

(She laughs. She then stands up, lifts her head and walks defiantly up to TOOD.)

SYBIL. *(Deliberately, cold)* We are modern.

(LIGHTS begin to fade. SYBIL runs off, TOOD follows her. WEETSIE is revealed upstage. She steps out of the shadows, watching the other women leave. She has been listening to the whole conversation. The LIGHTS fade.)

Scene Fourteen

(KATE, with an impressive camera, is taking photographs of

*the house, porch, etc. ADDIE MAE, with her small
camera, is taking pictures of KATE taking pictures.)*

ADDIE MAE. Now, Kate, give me a good pose. Right
there. Like we was taking pictures of each other!

KATE. *(Posing)* How's this?

ADDIE MAE. Great! Great! *(AUNT OLA enters with the
"bolero" top to SYBIL's sundress that we saw in SYBIL's
earlier monologue. She is sewing on a button)* Oooh! Aunt
Ola! Let me get you in a shot with Kate. For posterity!

KATE. Yes! For *Life* magazine!

AUNT OLA. *(Coming out to porch)* Lord, I ain't studyin'
Life magazine. *(Overcoming initial reluctance, she poses
grandly. KATE and ADDIE MAE take a snapshot. As AUNT
OLA continues in her pose, KATE and ADDIE MAE start to
move to another shot)* Hey! Now wait a minute, you done got
me interested. *(Enjoying this)* How 'bout one of me churnin'
butter? Or one showin' what the well-dressed country widder
wears to the outhouse?

KATE. Aunt Ola! You're not a widow.

AUNT OLA. There's all kinds of widders.

ADDIE MAE. Aunt Ola, one more! I'm makin' a
scrapbook of all these moments. What you makin', Aunt Ola?

AUNT OLA. Oh, all my little princesses got to have a
new dress for these pictures. And you know, I just board here.

ADDIE MAE. Let me go rustle up them girls!

(ADDIE MAE exits.)

KATE. Well, now it looks to me like you have on
something new there, too, Aunt Ola.

AUNT OLA. Just the cuffs and the collars. To bring out
the girl in me.

KATE. Speaking of the girl in you, Aunt Ola, how old are you?

AUNT OLA. Forty-six, come November.

(There is an obvious difference in the way the two women look. KATE has had no idea how young AUNT OLA is.)

KATE. Why, Aunt Ola, you're just a few years older than I am!

(Both women look at each other, commenting silently on the difference in their appearance.)

AUNT OLA. *(Finally)* Oh, Kate, it ain't the years, it's the miles. age isnt but a number?

(AUNT OLA smiles, exits. KATE watches her, and then turns, alone on stage, looks around.)

KATE. Oh, Aunt Ola, it ain't the miles, it's the terrain.

(ADDIE MAE enters with a chair.)

ADDIE MAE. The girls are comin'. Between these here pictures and the boys comin' home, why the excitement around here is so thick you could cut it with a knife. Nothin' ain't gonna be quite the same after you!

KATE. Why, thank you. I think. You know, I'm even getting excited about the boys coming home. They should start arriving any time.

ADDIE MAE. How in the world did y'all pull something like that off?

KATE. Harry. Knows everybody in the War Department by their first names.

ADDIE MAE:*(Amazed)* Huh. By their first names.

(WEETSIE and SYBIL emerge. WEETSIE is wearing a conservative summer frock. SYBIL is wearing the same sundress we saw in the earlier monologue.)

ADDIE MAE. Sybil, you sure know how to ... dress.

SYBIL. *(Modeling)* It's a whole outfit! Aunt Ola made it!

(KATE and ADDIE MAE take pictures as SYBIL and WEETSIE pose.)

KATE. Great. Let's try one with the two of you on the chair.

ADDIE MAE. Oh, goodness yes! *(Looks around)* Oh, we need Tood for this one.

SYBIL. She's supposed to be here. While we're waitin', I can change.

WEETSIE. Sybil, you have changed clothes three times.

SYBIL. *(Unconcerned)* So what?

WEETSIE. It's takin' a lot of time, Mrs. Miller has more important things to do than sit around waitin' for you to change clothes.

SYBIL. You're gettin' kinda pushy, ain't you? I liked you a whole lot better as the quiet little mousy thing you used to be. *(To KATE)* Kate, don't mind us. We love each other. I got a flashy little number I know you'll like.

KATE. *(Amused)* You go ahead, Sybil. It's all right. That's why I am here. To get the real story on the Cliffert family. Besides, I've got Addie Mae – chauffeur, secretary, postal clerk, typist – so you see, I *don't* have anything better to do.

ADDIE MAE. Well, imagine how it tickles me to help! *(Pointedly)* Now, y'all can't hog her for her entire stay. *(To KATE)* You got to spend some time with me and Sonny.

(SYBIL exits.)

WEETSIE. *(Sheepishly)* Did you write up the real story on the Cliffert family that first day when me and Sybil come in here like we was harpies? I ain't never been so embarrassed in my life!

KATE. It was fine.

WEETSIE. Did you squabble with your brothers and sisters?

KATE. Didn't have any. Just my mother and me.

WEETSIE. Oh, Mrs. Miller, it don't mean you ain't gonna put us on the cover of *Life* does it?

KATE. Not at all.

(SYBIL re-emerges in the dress JOHNNY bought her in New Orleans. A tight-fitting, but pretty summer dress.)

SYBIL. Tah-daah!
KATE. Lovely.
ADDIE MAE. Right out of *Harper's Bazaar!*

(Photo session continues with KATE and ADDIE MAE taking candid and posed shots through next section.)

WEETSIE. *(To SYBIL)* How come you can keep so skinny and eat everything that'll go through your shoulderblades?!

SYBIL. I don't sneak Aunt Ola's apple turnovers.

WEETSIE. *(Defiantly)* I ain't sneakin' nothin'. I just eat 'em outright.

SYBIL. Shameful.

WEETSIE. *(Pointedly)* I'd walk clear of me today, if I was you, Sybil. *(Proudly)* I ain't on no diet. I'm probably on my way to being the size of a barn, but I do not care. Repeat, do not.

SYBIL. What about your honey?

WEETSIE. It's my honey. And he loves me just the way I am.

SYBIL. Oh, come on, you 'spect he's dreamin' about comin' home to that? You ain't too smart.

WEETSIE. Sybil, I am smart enough to know Southern boys wants to marry their mammas.

SYBIL. *(Mockingly, to KATE)* Chubby and warm like a chenille bathrobe.

WEETSIE. Yeah. *(Takes control, fires off the next in a steady, confident stream)* That can cook collard greens and fry chicken and hang clothes out on the line while holdin' one youngun on one hip and lettin' the other suck a tit, keep a house so clean his *mamma* would eat off the floor, know the Bible backwards and forwards, know her place on the front porch and in the back room, gets to sit in the front seat on Sunday and by the telephone on Saturday night, wonderin' where he is and when he is gonna come home. But home he will come. Time after time. Now you might think I'm not so smart as somebody as sophisticated as you Sybil Louise Harrist with a "t", but the last I looked, I ain't received no Dear Sybil letter like some folks I know.

(SYBIL slaps WEETSIE hard across the face.)

WEETSIE. You and your big talk about being such a woman. Well, I'd like to know how you can be such a woman when you're as barren as the Sarah Desert!

(SYBIL is overcome by the tirade and the accuracy of WEETSIE's comment. The women all stand there for an uncomfortable moment. KATE has listened to the whole thing with her camera at the ready and snaps the camera just as WEETSIE finishes her speech. The young women are caught in their embarrassment. It is too late.)

KATE. *(Trying to smooth over the uncomfortable situation)* Look ... uh ... uh ... why don't we do some more of this later? I promised Addie Mae she could show me a real live bayou! *(Searching)* Isn't that right, Addie Mae?

ADDIE MAE. *(Caught by surprise)* Oh, *lord yes*! Cypress knees! Moss!

KATE. *(Still trying to ease the situation)* A bayou! I couldn't miss that. People up North ask me if y'all have webbed feet because of the bayous! *(Hears herself. Laughs)* Ohmigod, "Y'all." *(Pause, to herself)* I gotta get back to New York!

(KATE starts to exit.)

ADDIE MAE. Let me say good-bye to Aunt Ola. It would just break her heart if I didn't say good-bye. *(Calls out as she exits)* Aunt Ola! Aunt Ola!

(There is an uncomfortable silence. KATE realizes the tenseness of the situation.)

KATE. *(Eager to comfort SYBIL)* Sybil, honey, there are worse things than ... uh, listen, why don't you –

SYBIL. *(Sharply)* I ain't worried about that letter. It's just a temporary lapse in Johnny's eternal devotion to me.

KATE. There then. It's gonna be fine.

SYBIL. It just comes with understandin' your man. *(Coming around)* Besides, I done got another letter. *(Pulls out blue envelope)* See, Weetsie? Me and Johnny is always a step ahead of you.

WEETSIE. *(Still defiantly)* Well, that was quick, wasn't it? Why didn't you tell us?

SYBIL. Because I want to savor it all for myself. *For once.*

WEETSIE. Well, I'm glad for you, Sybil.

SYBIL. Right. Don't worry, Weetsie, I don't never pay no attention to you anyway. *(Faltering a bit. Then, directly to KATE)* I'm just waitin'. *(Then to herself)* Waitin' and wishin', just like everybody else.

(SYBIL runs off, the other women watch her. TOOD enters from the other side of the stage, bedraggled, exhausted, furious.)

WEETSIE. Tood, what in the world happened to you?

TOOD. Where do you want me to start? I was doin' wash when I run out of bluin'. So, I had to go to town. Well, Lloyd and Lois come by here and Lois said they had to go to town too, so I could ride with them. I didn't want to, but I did. But Lloyd had to go pick up some duck decoys he was buyin' out on the Crossett Highway. And we get there and he asked Lois for his billfold, which she was supposed to have in her purse.

WEETSIE. *(Interrupting)* Brother don't like to carry a

billfold. *(TOOD looks at WEETSIE incredulously. WEETSIE explains to KATE)* When he drives, it hurts his behind.

TOOD. *(Continues the story)* Well, she didn't have the billfold. And you ain't gonna believe this. He told her to walk home and get it.

KATE. What?

TOOD. *(Astounded)* Yes! It was might near ten miles!

WEETSIE. What did you do?

TOOD. I struck out with her.

WEETSIE. Tood, you're pregnant!

TOOD. So what? I sure wasn't gonna stay there with Lloyd. And then after about three miles he comes along and makes Lois get in the truck, because *(Mocking Lloyd)* "he reckoned she had learned a lesson now."

KATE. That sonofabitch.

TOOD. And he tells me to get in too. And I shake my head "no" and I keep walkin'. And he's tellin' me I better do what he tells me or he's gonna tell Teat. And I keep walkin'.

WEETSIE. Oh Lord, I bet he's mad.

KATE. To hell with Lloyd.

TOOD. Lord in heaven, why does that woman take that? She is just the best old soul and as soon as she couldn't find her purse, she started squallin' and shakin'.

(A truck HORN is heard, blowing incessantly. WEETSIE looks out, alarmed.)

WEETSIE. Oh my god. It's Lloyd.

(HORN continues to blow. TOOD is growing angrier, but doesn't move. WEETSIE is apoplectic. Everyone stands still, not knowing what to do. Finally, KATE moves forward and yells, loudly.)

KATE. *GODDAMN you Lloyd Cliffert, you are disturbing the peace!*

TOOD. *(Taking up the gauntlet uncertainly)* Yeah. *(Then stronger)* Yeah!

KATE. *Take your goddamn truck ...*

TOOD. *(Into it) ... and your stupid grin ...*

KATE. *... and get the hell out of here!*

TOOD. *Go ahead and laugh! You ... uh ... stupid hyena!* *(KATE reacts to TOOD's choice of derision. KATE joins in) Stupid hyena! Stupid hyena! Stupid hyena!*

WEETSIE. Y'all, stop it!

TOOD & KATE. *Stupid hyena! Stupid hyena!*

(HORN stops as the SOUND of LLOYD's truck driving off is heard. WEETSIE looks uneasily at TOOD, who is shocked at her own boldness. KATE smiles and shakes her head.)

WEETSIE. *(To TOOD, gravely)* I wouldn't want to be in your shoes now.

TOOD. I don't know Weetsie, my shoes feel pretty good right now. *(TOOD and KATE smile at each other. WEETSIE looks at KATE and TOOD disapprovingly, then goes into the house. KATE and TOOD look at each other and begin to laugh. TOOD enjoys the moment, reliving her triumph) Stupid hyena! Stupid hyena!*

(KATE quickly takes a snapshot of TOOD.)

KATE. In your moment of glory!

TOOD. Don't you dare! Look at me!

(TOOD chases KATE playfully, trying to wrest the camera from her as KATE continues taking photos.)

KATE. Come on! A wife left behind!

TOOD. I look like something the dog's dug up! *(KATE laughs)* Now you don't want to make a country gal mad. Gimme that camera! Gimme that camera!

(KATE laughs, runs into the house with TOOD following her. LIGHTS fade.)

Scene Fifteen

(SYBIL is alone on stage, holding an airmail envelope.)

SYBIL. I got your second letter. It come so fast I knew it must be good news. I was walkin' to town and I passed Femmie Musgrove and I waved the little, blue envelope at him, hollerin' "I got a letter from *him* today. From my honey!" You know, Femmie Musgrove would walk through a wasp nest just to hold my hand. Then I opened my little, light blue, paper valentine. And it was bluer than I thought. I was too weak to make it to town. There was a car parked by the side of the road, so I sat down on the runnin' board and I read my blue valentine again. *(A desperate challenge, but with her trademark sardonic sense of humor)* So. I guess you found you a whole woman on the other side of the moon. Why didn't you tell me the real truth in the first letter? Huh? Are you and her gonna call it Little Johnny? Oh god, I thought that was one of the reasons you wanted me. I was a woman as hot as a Saturday night and as safe as Sunday mornin'. But I wasn't no *real* woman, was I, Johnny? I'm as barren as the Sahara Desert. And now everybody's gonna find out. Hell, it's gonna be on the cover of *Life* magazine. *(More somber)* Oh, Johnny. I love you. I ain't ever even looked at another man. Not ever. Not once. I ain't nothin' without you. I guess you told me that so many times that I finally believe it. I guess you don't make her feel like nothin', huh? She has her womanhood. *(Following speech begins with control, with an almost naive puzzlement)* You know, I told Tood I didn't believe in dreams. But I lied. *(Matter-of-factly)* I give *you* all my dreams. All at once. I took the ones I carry around in my purse, and I give 'em to you. I found some I hid, and I give 'em to you. Hell, I had some brand new ones, and I just up and give 'em to you. Cause you could do something fine with all them dreams. *(Anger taking over)* Well, what did you do with them? Huh? Are they in your knapsack over there? Or did you take them and trade them in on something bigger and better? *(An eruption of fear and fury)* WHERE IN THE HELL ARE MY DREAMS? *(Rage)* YOU HAVE ABANDONED ME HERE ON DONALDSON STREET, STERLINGTON, LOUISIANA, USA, WITHOUT A DREAM IN SIGHT! AND THE WHOLE WORLD IS GONNA KNOW. GODDAMN *LIFE* MAGAZINE HAS ITS NOSE UP MY BEHIND, WRITIN' DOWN EVER' TIME I PEE! WELL, I DON'T WANT MY UNDERWEAR HUNG OUT TO DRY FROM COAST TO COAST! I DON'T WANT THE WHOLE WORLD TO KNOW ABOUT MY WOMANHOOD! DO YOU HEAR? DO YOU HEAR? *(Almost as if she is looking around for them)* WHERE IN THE HELL ARE MY DREAMS? *(Suddenly very meek)* I'm sorry. I'm sorry, Baby. I'm sorry. I didn't mean to make such a fuss. *(Models dress)* See this? You bought this for me in

New Orleans. You said ... you said ... *(Almost breaks down, but then becomes very matter-of-fact)* What the hell difference does it make what you said?

(Sound of GUNSHOT as LIGHTS fade.)

Scene Sixteen

(TOOD is on stage, looking out. WEETSIE comes to her. KATE is now at ADDIE MAE's home as indicated by the different telephone and its location. KATE moves to the telephone. She is very upset, overcome.)

WEETSIE. Tood? I get such an ache.
TOOD. Shhh. I know. I know.
WEETSIE. Hold me, Tood. I'm scared.
KATE. Harry? *(Somehow distracted)* Uh ... Harry? Something's happened. *(Almost breaks down)* We have to pull the story.
WEETSIE. Tood, do you think she lost her mind?
TOOD. I 'spect so, Weetsie, I 'spect so. Now, you go on and get ready.

(TOOD kisses WEETSIE on the forehead. WEETSIE exits. TOOD moves down stage, very near KATE, although they are in different places.)

KATE. *(Finding it very difficult to tell the story)* Uh ... Harry ... Sybil ... *(Privately, looking out)* Oh god, Sybil. *(Back to phone)* You can't go with what I've sent you. *(Angry)* Don't tell me it's too late! You own the goddamn thing. Harry, this is a real story now.

TOOD. *(Overwhelmed by the heartbreak and horror of it)* Oh, Tommy, Sybil used Uncle Tom's pistol.

KATE. Yes, and christ, Harry, the father died less than twenty-four hours later, peacefully in his sleep. *Peacefully.*

TOOD. Peacefully in his sleep.

KATE. That's irony for you isn't it? *(Bitterly angry)* This poor girl blows out her insides, and he goes in his sleep. Jesus.

TOOD. Tommy, she placed the barrel up inside her and pulled the trigger. She done it that way on purpose. To take revenge on the source of her failure.

KATE. She left a note, addressed to Tood. It said only, "What is wrong with my womanhood?"

TOOD. What is wrong with my womanhood.

KATE. *(Regaining control)* Harry, Harry. That's the story.

TOOD. They give Aunt Ola the gun 'cause they said it wasn't no murder weapon. But it was a murder weapon. Johnny murdered her. And Lloyd. And ...

KATE. What? How do I feel ... about what? This place? Sybil? Uncle Tom? What? Hell, I don't know. I guess I'm putting it all on three by five cards ... as always. But I don't want to. *I want to explode with rage. God, Harry, aren't there any times in your life when your goddamn civility goes out the goddamn window? (Starts to cry)* Harry, please, pull the story. Please. Please.

(LIGHTS fade on KATE.)

Scene Seventeen

(TOOD is in the living room. ADDIE MAE arrives at door carrying two covered dishes, and magazines clamped

under her arm. She is overdressed in effusively funereal attire. TOOD lets her in. ADDIE MAE puts dishes down.)

ADDIE MAE. *(The professional mourner)* Oh, you are all just angels! My heart is just absolutely broken. Shattered. Two deaths in the same house within twenty-four hours of each other. Tragic. Angels.

TOOD. *(Unmoved)* Thank you, Addie Mae. *(Looks out the door)* Have you seen Kate?

ADDIE MAE. Yes, Baby, she's got her stuff at my house. We're gonna take her to Monroe to the train tonight.

TOOD. Didn't she even plan to say good-bye?

ADDIE MAE. Here. I brought these.

(Hands magazines to TOOD.)

TOOD. *(Confused, disbelief)* These are copies of *Collier's* magazine.

ADDIE MAE. Yes. They ran an entire series of articles on grief when Clark Gable lost Carole Lombard! They were a great comfort to my mamma when my daddy died. Can I see Aunt Ola? I also brought a covered dish – a banana puddin'. Actually, I brought two. *(Deep reverence)* One for Sybil and ... *(Deeper reverence)* one for Uncle Tom.

(A LOUD CRASH OF DISHES BREAKING is heard from OFFSTAGE.)

AUNT OLA. *(Offstage)* Weetsie! Get the hell out of my kitchen!

WEETSIE. *(Rushing out from the kitchen)* Tood! Tood! Aunt Ola has lost her mind!

AUNT OLA. *(Entering right behind WEETSIE, carrying the pistol)* Out! Out! *(Sees ADDIE MAE)* What the hell are you doin' here?

ADDIE MAE. Oh my god, she's got a gun!

AUNT OLA. If it wasn't for you, this whole mess wouldn't have started in the first place!

(ADDIE MAE runs off when AUNT OLA starts toward her.)

ADDIE MAE. *(Not knowing where to run)* She's got a gun! She's got a gun!

WEETSIE. *(Cowering behind TOOD)* She was in the kitchen talkin' to Uncle Tom, and breakin' up dishes with the handle of that godawful pistol!

AUNT OLA. I wasn't breakin' up my dishes, I was breakin' up Tom's. They ain't no use to Tom now, are they Weetsie?

TOOD. Aunt Ola!

AUNT OLA. Weetsie, you in such a twist to start mournin', get on down to the funeral home and get 'em all worked up for when I walk in. Now! I didn't stutter.

(WEETSIE runs out. AUNT OLA sneaks a knowing look at TOOD, hiding a smile.)

AUNT OLA. *(Turning to ADDIE MAE, "absent-mindedly" pointing gun at her as she gestures)* And you!

ADDIE MAE. *(Alarmed)* Me?

AUNT OLA. You and your goddamn newspaper, comin' in here, stirrin' things up.

ADDIE MAE. All I've stirred up is the truth. I reckon you ain't to blame for nothin'. Humph! People always is blamin' the press!

people react different to grief

*(ADDIE MAE sashays off. AUNT OLA watches her, smiles to
    herself, shakes her head.)*

AUNT OLA. *(Mimicking)* People is always blamin' the
press! *(TOOD and AUNT OLA laugh, both understanding the
moment. Then as laughter subsides, still lightly, but in a more
serious vein)* Tood, what do you think of me?

TOOD. I love you, Aunt Ola.

AUNT OLA. Don't talk to me like Weetsie.

TOOD. *(Small smile)* I didn't say I wanted to *be* you,
Aunt Ola.

AUNT OLA. And ... call me Ola. *(Begins pacing around
the room)* Do you know it's been nearly thirty years since
anybody called me Ola. Just Ola. Oh, every now and then
Tom would call me Ola if he wanted to scare me. *(She picks
up photograph of boys and throws it on a chair.)*

TOOD. Ola, what are you doin'?

AUNT OLA. *(Looking around, considering the question)*
I don't know, baby. I'm just doin' something. *(Realizing her
options are many)* Sure as hell ain't gonna be no man around
here now. I'm just doin' something. Hell, I might move that
old chair over yonder ... to ... over yonder. That was Tom's
chair. *(Mocking, Pappa Bear voice)* The big chair. And
Tom's chair went by the window so's he could see to read the
newspaper, and look out at people passin' by and such as that.
You know, you can't see a damn thing from my kitchen
window. All them years I looked out at nothin' but that
damned half-acre field. *(Puts picture back)* There. Ain't no
sense in throwin' it away just yet.

TOOD. Ola, them is your boys.

AUNT OLA. Whoop-de-do. Anyways I'm tired of being
somebody's mamma.

(Pause. AUNT OLA looks at the pistol for a long moment.)

TOOD. Ola?

AUNT OLA. I been thinkin' about Sybil. Killed herself with Tom's pistol. *(Overcome, confused)* What am I? What have I been? *(Amazed at herself)* He couldn't clean it after he shot himself with it ... so ... *I* did it. I cleaned and oiled and ... I just *did* it. Didn't question it at all. So when Sybil took it, it was in perfect workin' condition. Perfect workin' condition. Maybe if it hadn't been in perfect workin' condition, Sybil would still be here.

TOOD. Aunt Ola, you didn't have nothin' to do with that.

AUNT OLA. *(Furious)* STOP IT! STOP IT! What am I? You are right – I didn't have nothin' to do with it. Cause I didn't do nothin'. But sit and take and fix supper and clean slop jars *(Looks toward TOM's chair)* and let them boys think their daddy could do no wrong. *(Strongly to the absent TOM)* Politics and fishin'! I just stood in front of that damn stove while they turned into their daddy.

TOOD. Not Tommy!

AUNT OLA. *(Defiantly)* I started out a good woman with a big heart. We all do. And I *loved* Tom Cliffert. But love ain't enough. Love can't change character. *(Sadly)* But my boys. My boys. *(Starts to falter)* I give them just enough of me so that another good woman would fall in love with them. But they got the biggest part from their daddy. And I let it happen. I didn't fight.

TOOD. Ola, don't.

AUNT OLA. *(She begins to fight back tears as TOOD comes to her)* My boys has all got blue eyes *(Looks at TOOD desperately)* ... and black hearts, too.

(Pause as we see TOOD come to a decision.)

TOOD. Aunt Ola, don't worry. Me and Tommy won't ever leave you.

(AUNT OLA looks at TOOD puzzledly. A pause as AUNT OLA comes to a decision of her own. AUNT OLA hands TOOD the gun.)

AUNT OLA. Here, take this. Keep it someplace important. The boys'll claim it as theirs, but it's mine and I'm givin' it to you. You take Tommy and you get out of here. And use this – it's gotta be worth *something.* Maybe you can do better by him than me.

TOOD. *(Taking the gun with uncertainty)* Ola, I don't know what to do with this gun.

AUNT OLA. Well, *figure it out.* The men did. *(Pause, change)* Now. You go on. *(Sarcastically)* I got to go be the good widderwoman in a little while. But before I do, I am gonna sit right here and take a long, easy look out of this window.

(AUNT OLA sits in the chair and looks out of the window. TOOD looks at the pistol, moves to the front porch.)

Scene Eighteen

TOOD. *(On porch. TOOD caresses pistol, almost as if it were a token of SYBIL)* Oh, Sybil, I love you. *(Puts pistol away.)*

(KATE enters dressed to depart, carrying luggage, etc. Goes to TOOD. KATE and TODD look at each other for a long moment before KATE speaks.)

KATE. Hey.

TOOD. I didn't even think you was gonna say good-bye! I thought, well, she's got her story ... on to the next ... scoop.

KATE. Ooh, that's pretty mean. Besides, Tood, you're the scoop.

TOOD. Right. *(Suddenly very direct, firm)* You got to help me. *(They hug)* The hurricane's gettin' closer.

KATE. You mean Tommy?

TOOD. I can't face him. *(Really frightened, looking out. Very directly)* You got to take me with you. I am smart and pretty and I can find work. I won't be no burden.

KATE. Tood, you know I can't do that.

TOOD. *No, I don't know that.* I won't take up no room! I can sleep sittin' up in a straight back chair.

KATE. Tood, you can't run away.

TOOD. Why not? It looks easy when you do it. Pack a bag. Catch a train. Run.

KATE. Stop this. You are not being fair!

TOOD. Fair?! Fair?! Do you think it's fair to abandon me here?

KATE. You are not my responsibility. Now ... I'm leaving. *(Starts to leave.)*

TOOD. Kate! You know that old sayin', "I can't hear myself think?"

KATE. Yeah.

TOOD. I used to say that all the time.

KATE. Me, too.

TOOD. Then you show up in your high-heels, and big shoulders. And you talk to me and you *listen* to me, and NOW I CAN'T DO ANYTHING BUT HEAR MYSELF THINK.

KATE. Well, what is wrong with that?

TOOD. I am stuck with it! And you have got to take some blame!

(The two women look at each other for a long silence, the comment just made has tremendous implications for both of them. KATE is unable to speak, tries to move toward TOOD, just as TOMMY enters with his duffel bag.)

TOMMY. Hey! You still my honey?

(TOOD sees him. She is suddenly immobile, between KATE and TOMMY. He runs up to her and spins her around.)

TOOD. Aunt Ola! Aunt Ola!

(TOMMY puts TOOD down and moves to AUNT OLA. TOOD stands center stage between AUNT OLA, TOMMY and KATE, looking at KATE.)

KATE. Just remember Tood, you see fine. *(Filled with sadness)* Good-bye, Tood.

(KATE exits. LIGHTS fade on all, as stage becomes bare.)

Scene Nineteen

(A deserted railroad track near the Cliffert house. It is later that same night. Nearly dawn. It is the soft blue darkness of MOONLIGHT. TOMMY and TOOD enter, moving cautiously, alone on stage. He is in his sailor uniform. They are looking for the mysterious "lantern light" to appear on the abandoned railroad track.)

TOMMY. Shhh. You gotta be real quiet if you want to see it. He comes out right before dawn.

TOOD. It ain't no dead man with a lantern looking for his head.

TOMMY. It is. Shhhh. You know that watchman got run over by the train right there. And they never found his head. *(Pause)* Boo!

TOOD. *(Startled)* Stop it! I know this old story. But I don't believe in ghosts. *(Uncertain)* Besides, that light people see is just natural gas or something.

TOMMY. They found his torso over yonder. And arms and legs over yonder. *(TOMMY is really "into" telling the story, TOOD is wide-eyed, looking around)* And now he comes out here ever' night lookin' for his head. *(TOMMY looks around too)* There it is!

TOOD. *(Jumping in fright)* Where? You don't see it. I know you don't!

TOMMY. If you're scared, I'll hold your hand.

TOOD. *(Smiling, playful)* I'm so scared you gonna have to do more'n hold my hand.

TOMMY. Well, in that case, let me see if I can get you plumb petrified.

(They laugh and embrace. Kiss passionately.)

TOOD. *(Silence, she turns away)* Was you proud of the money I saved? You know, I figured it up. Why, in just a year we're gonna have over three hundred dollars.

TOMMY. Damn.

TOOD. When this war is over, we could start our own business, or you could go to business school or ...

TOMMY. Hush, now. You workin' too hard. You gettin' too serious. Your sailor-boy just wants to dance.

TOOD. Tommy, honey, we got to do *some* serious talkin'.

TOMMY. Hell, Tood. We just been to two funerals, ain't that serious enough? Now, hush.

TOOD. *(Perplexed)* I'm sorry, baby, I can't *hush.* *(Seriously)* This is my life too, and I want to do some serious talkin'.

TOMMY. Something happened to you while I was gone. You ain't never talked this way before.

TOOD. Well, I talk this way now. *(Directly at TOMMY)* Things change.

TOMMY. That woman from *Life* magazine got you all pumped up, didn't she? Lloyd said she wasn't nothin' but a piece of shit wrapped up in a ten-dollar bill.

TOOD. Don't talk about her that way! Besides, I been askin' questions long before I heard from *Life* magazine.

TOMMY. What kind of questions?

TOOD. I don't know. Why? Why this? And why that? And why do I have to live next to your mamma all my life?!

TOMMY. *(Getting angry)* Oh, now I reckon there's something wrong with my mamma?

TOOD. No! There ain't nothin' wrong with your mamma. Don't you understand? Besides, baby, your mamma agrees with me one hundred percent.

TOMMY. Goddammit, Tood, what about me? I know what you want. You want us to leave here and if I leave here, I won't ever get any respect from them.

TOOD. If you *don't* leave here, you won't ever get any respect from them. Or me. You'll be Teat all your life.

TOMMY. Stop it, Tood! Don't do this.

TOOD. You'll be sellin' minnows and worms for Lloyd for the rest of your life. For Lloyd! Little Teat titty-baby!

(TOMMY pulls back his arm to strike her, catches himself. He is flushed with anger, but is horrified that he almost hit

*TOOD. She stands firmly and looks him in the eye. He
moves away from her.)*

TOMMY. I woulda never married you in the first place if
I paid any attention to Lloyd.

TOOD. *(Angry)* Maybe Lloyd was right.

TOMMY. I love you, Tood.

TOOD. I know you do. But, Baby, love is a livin' thing.
It dies. And it can be killed. Around here. Sybil loved Johnny.
Lois loved Lloyd. Aunt Ola loved Uncle Tom. But now ... all
that love is six-foot underground. I know you understand
exactly what I am sayin'.

TOMMY. Can't you give me a chance?

TOOD. If you really want a chance. *(Pause. This is
difficult for TOOD to bring up)* Tommy? What did you do
with the ninety-seven dollars I showed you last night? I went
in to get it a while ago. I had three more dollars to add to it. I
couldn't wait. It was gonna be a hundred dollars even.

TOMMY. Tood ...

TOOD. A hundred dollars. I been dreamin' about that
first hundred dollars since the first load of wash I done. And I
went there and it was gone.

TOMMY. *(He is embarrassed)* I took it.

TOOD. *(Very firmly, knowing the answer)* And what did
you do with it?

TOMMY. *(Long pause, embarrassed)* I give it to Lloyd.

TOOD. *(Firmly, evenly)* Go get it back.

TOMMY. Tood ...

TOOD. Now. That is my money too! That is *our* money!
You had no right!

TOMMY. Stop it!

TOOD. *THAT MONEY IS NOT A GODDAMN DOWN-
PAYMENT ON THE GODDAMN CLIFFERT BROTHERS*

BAIT AND GODDAMN TACKLE COMPANY! Go get it back! Oh Tommy, don't be a man for *them.* Be a man for *me. Fight* for me. Go get it back. For us. For the three of us.

(Long pause. They look at each other. This is the moment of heartbreak.)

TOMMY. *(Finally, fully aware of the implications of what he is saying, TOMMY speaks)* I can't. *(After a long moment, sadly, pleading with TOOD for her understanding)* I can't.

(TOOD looks at TOMMY. Her heart is broken. The LIGHT has changed to dawn breaking. Neither speaks for a long time. There is a glass wall between them. They look through the glass with love, resignation.)

TOMMY. *(Finally)* Dance with me. Dance with me.

(LIGHTS fade on them.)

Epilogue

(KATE enters holding a copy of Life.*)*

KATE. *(Addresses audience)* Well, as it turned out, *Life* magazine waited for no one. Harry still swears he was unable to stop the issue in time. He got his woman's piece just as he wanted it. I changed trains in Atlanta and stopped in a newsstand for a pack of cigarettes. And there they were. Beaming across the cover of *Life. (*Life *cover with the three*

wives saluting appears in a large projection or TOOD, SYBIL
and WEETSIE appear in tableau reminiscent of Scene 1 pose)
The photograph wasn't even one of mine. It was one of Addie
Mae's. *(KATE clutches the magazine to her)* I turned in my
resignation to Harry as soon as I got back. He refused it,
saying that I was acting just like a woman. "Damn right," I
said. And I began asking questions. Like why? Why this and
why that? And why do I have to work for Harry Luce all my
life?

(Finally, KATE opens letter slowly. She reads it)

TOOD. *(Voice over)* Uncle Tom's pistol was worth
$475.00. That can keep you goin'. I seen a poster at the library
for a book by somebody named Kate Miller. They ain't got it
in yet, but when I seen the title, I knew it was you. *Hearing
Myself Think.* I reckon we're both stuck with that, huh? Love,
Tood.

KATE. *(To TOOD)* I told you I'd make it up to you.
(Back to audience) When I left the magazine, this is the only
thing I took with me. And I look at it every day, and every day
it gives me purpose.

(LIGHTS fade on KATE and then the projection/tableau.)

THE END

SETTING

The set does not take precedence in THE COVER OF LIVE. Instead the areas are defined by set pieces such as the table and chairs for the dining area, the clothesline, the telephone and the chair for Uncle Tom. The props, such as the laundry or the food, help to further ground the action. The author wants no realistic framework *(flats, walls, etc.)* to confine the action to a place or time.

PROPS

ACT I *(On-stage)*
    Phone
        - candlestick in SL cubby
        - Rotary in SR cubby on
           Steno pad w/pencil
           in wire rings
    Porch down

ACT I *(Trap)*

    Bench

Off Stage

Up Center
    Registered letter
    1 glass w/iced tea
    Plate w/coconut cake
    Fork *(attached to plate)*
    Telephone
    Ashtray w/water

ACT II
    Glass w/water
    Plate w/cornbread
    2 cups water
    Chair

Shelf URC
    1 glass of iced tea (¼ full)
    Coffee cup
    Lighter
    1 Kate cigarette

Stage Right
    2 Chairs
        1 cut to rake w/Tood pad & pencil set on UR ramp
        1 flat in hall
    Sybil's purse w/compact, lipstick, lighter, cigarettes
        (preset in cup by purse) pad, pencil, picture
    Perfume
    Addie Mae's camera
    Addie Mae's purse w/hanky
    Kate's small notepad and pen
    Extra Tood to Kate letter
    Life magazine
    3 allotment checks
    Sears Roebuck catalogue
    Letter – Johnny to Sybil – unopened with heart
    Letter – Jerry Don to Ola in envelope – opened
    Weetsie's pad and pencil
    Letter – Tood to Tommy
    Camera bag – ½ opened – camera handle up, front end
        toward front – w/1 film
    Suitcase
    Briefcase
    Bag w/Tripod
    Small bag for Weetsie
    Cigarettes
    Lighter

Kate's portfolio with clippings, pad and 2 pencils
Liquor bottle full
Champagne glass
Letter – Tommy to Tood – opened with heart
Washtub w/wash board and 1 shirt
Garment *(Ola to fold)*
Green bean tub
Johnny letter #1 – opened
Johnny letter #2 – unopened with heart
Weetsie's crocheting
Light meter and 4 films *(set in vest)*
2 covered dishes
Collier's magazines
1 framed photo of 3 brothers
Small travel bag
Duffel bag
Sewing basket with Ola's crocheting and Ola's glasses

Off Stage Left
Clothesline with clothes
Shirt with own clothespins
Clothespins in small bag – attached to line
Laundry basket empty
Laundry basket with damp clothes
Letter – Tood to Kate with envelope unopened
Tray with
    3 plates with 3 forks & 3 napkins
    1 plate with 1 fork & 1 napkin
    4 glasses iced tea
    Cornbread w/knife
Bowl of black eyed peas w/spoon
3x5 cards and pencil

Colander with green beans
Letter – Tood to Tommy – opened
Picnic basket with:
    Thermos w/ "coffee"
    2 cups
    2 apple turnovers in 2 napkins
Letter – Sybil to Johnny unopened in envelope
Gun
1 Framed photograph of 3 brothers
2 Chairs
    1 cut to rake
    1 flat

THE COVER OF LIFE

COSTUME

KATE:
> ACT I
>> (Scenes 1, 2, 5) Green Suit, blouse, black pumps
>> (Scene 7) Navy pant suit, blouse, same pumps
>> (Scene 10) Rust pants suit, blouse, brown pumps
>> (Scene 11) Robe and slippers
>
> ACT II
>> (Scene 12, 14) Rust suit, blouse, brown pumps
>> (Scene 16, 18) Navy suit, blouse, black pumps
>> (Epilogue) Green skirt suit, black shoes

ADDIE MAE:
> ACT I
>> (Scene 2) Robe, curlers, net, slippers
>> (Scene 8) Green & purple print rayon dress, green opened toed shoes
>
> ACT II
>> (Scene 14) Same as Scene 8 w/Flat enclosed sandal style shoes, green handbag
>> (Scene 17) Navy blue rayon dress, black flat shoes, gloves, purse, navy hat

TOOD:
> ACT I
>> (Scene 1, 2, 3, 4, 6, 7) Blue gray & turquoise small print cotton shirtwaist dress, flat open back, light colored shoes, add apron in Scene 2
>> (Scene 8, 10, 11) Blue cotton dress, same shoes

TOOD: *(cont.)*
ACT II
    (Scene 12, 13, 14) Blue cotton dress, no shoes
    (Scene 16, 17, 18) Black shirt waist dress, black low heeled dress shoes
    (Scene 19, Epilogue) First dress and shoes

SYBIL:
ACT I
    (Scene 3, 4) Purple skirt, navy crop top, open back shoes
    (Scene 7) Full skirt, short tie in front top, clutch purse, open backed shoes
    (Scene 9, 11) Stars and stripes red, white and blue low bodice dress, same shoes
ACT II
    (Scene 13) Purple skirt, navy crop top, sandals
    (Scene 14) Red, white and blue dress from Act I – Very sexy silky rayon tight fitting straight skirt dress
    (Scene 15) Silky rayon dress

WEETSIE:
ACT I
    (Scene 3, 4, 5) Pink & gray frumpy dress, closed tie up shoes
    (Scene 7, 8, 11) Red and gray dress, same shoes
ACT II
    (Scene 13) Robe, gown, slippers
    (Scene 14) Blue leaf print dress (more fitted than her others)
    (Scene 16) Black dress, dress shoes, hat, gloves, purse

AUNT OLA:
> ACT I
>> (Scene 3) Blue and white house dress, closed light colored shoes, apron
>> (Scene 8) Purple and pink house dress, same shoes
>> (Scene 11) Green, red and peach print house dress, same shoes, apron
>
> ACT II
>> (Scene 14) Dress with cuffs and collars, dress sandals
>> (Scene 17) Black dress, dress shoes

TOMMY:
> Sailor suit

SKIN DEEP
Jon Lonoff

Comedy / 2m, 2f / Interior Unit Set

In *Skin Deep*, a large, lovable, lonely-heart, named Maureen Mulligan, gives romance one last shot on a blind-date with sweet awkward Joseph Spinelli; she's learned to pepper her speech with jokes to hide insecurities about her weight and appearance, while he's almost dangerously forthright, saying everything that comes to his mind. They both know they're perfect for each other, and in time they come to admit it.

They were set up on the date by Maureen's sister Sheila and her husband Squire, who are having problems of their own: Sheila undergoes a non-stop series of cosmetic surgeries to hang onto the attractive and much-desired Squire, who may or may not have long ago held designs on Maureen, who introduced him to Sheila. With Maureen particularly vulnerable to both hurting and being hurt, the time is ripe for all these unspoken issues to bubble to the surface.

"Warm-hearted comedy … the laughter was literally show-stopping. A winning play, with enough good-humored laughs and sentiment to keep you smiling from beginning to end."
– *TalkinBroadway.com*

"It's a little Paddy Chayefsky, a lot Neil Simon and a quick-witted, intelligent voyage into the not-so-tranquil seas of middle-aged love and dating. The dialogue is crackling and hilarious; the plot simple but well-turned; the characters endearing and quirky; and lurking beneath the merriment is so much heartache that you'll stand up and cheer when the unlikely couple makes it to the inevitable final clinch."
– *NYTheatreWorld.Com*

SAMUELFRENCH.COM

TREASURE ISLAND
Ken Ludwig

All Groups / Adventure / 10m, 1f (doubling) / Areas
Based on the masterful adventure novel by Robert Louis Stevenson, *Treasure Island* is a stunning yarn of piracy on the tropical seas. It begins at an inn on the Devon coast of England in 1775 and quickly becomes an unforgettable tale of treachery and mayhem featuring a host of legendary swashbucklers including the dangerous Billy Bones (played unforgettably in the movies by Lionel Barrymore), the sinister two-timing Israel Hands, the brassy woman pirate Anne Bonney, and the hideous form of evil incarnate, Blind Pew. At the center of it all are Jim Hawkins, a 14-year-old boy who longs for adventure, and the infamous Long John Silver, who is a complex study of good and evil, perhaps the most famous hero-villain of all time. Silver is an unscrupulous buccaneer-rogue whose greedy quest for gold, coupled with his affection for Jim, cannot help but win the heart of every soul who has ever longed for romance, treasure and adventure.

THE OFFICE PLAYS
Two full length plays by Adam Bock

THE RECEPTIONIST
Comedy / 2m, 2f / Interior

At the start of a typical day in the Northeast Office, Beverly deals effortlessly with ringing phones and her colleague's romantic troubles. But the appearance of a charming rep from the Central Office disrupts the friendly routine. And as the true nature of the company's business becomes apparent, The Receptionist raises disquieting, provocative questions about the consequences of complicity with evil.

"...Mr. Bock's poisoned Post-it note of a play."
– *New York Times*

"Bock's intense initial focus on the routine goes to the heart of *The Receptionist's* pointed, painfully timely allegory... elliptical, provocative play..."
– *Time Out New York*

THE THUGS
Comedy / 2m, 6f / Interior

The Obie Award winning dark comedy about work, thunder and the mysterious things that are happening on the 9th floor of a big law firm. When a group of temps try to discover the secrets that lurk in the hidden crevices of their workplace, they realize they would rather believe in gossip and rumors than face dangerous realities.

"Bock starts you off giggling, but leaves you with a chill."
– *Time Out New York*

"... a delightfully paranoid little nightmare that is both more chillingly realistic and pointedly absurd than anything John Grisham ever dreamed up."
– *New York Times*

SAMUELFRENCH.COM

WHITE BUFFALO
Don Zolidis

Drama / 3m, 2f (plus chorus)/ Unit Set

Based on actual events, WHITE BUFFALO tells the story of the miracle birth of a white buffalo calf on a small farm in southern Wisconsin. When Carol Gelling discovers that one of the buffalo on her farm is born white in color, she thinks nothing more of it than a curiosity. Soon, however, she learns that this is the fulfillment of an ancient prophecy believed by the Sioux to bring peace on earth and unity to all mankind. Her little farm is quickly overwhelmed with religious pilgrims, bringing her into contact with a culture and faith that is wholly unfamiliar to her. When a mysterious businessman offers to buy the calf for two million dollars, Carol is thrown into doubt about whether to profit from the religious beliefs of others or to keep true to a spirituality she knows nothing about.

BLUE YONDER
Kate Aspengren

Dramatic Comedy / Monolgues and scenes
12f (can be performed with as few as 4 with doubling) / Unit Set

A familiar adage states, "Men may work from sun to sun, but women's work is never done." In Blue Yonder, the audience meets twelve mesmerizing and eccentric women including a flight instructor, a firefighter, a stuntwoman, a woman who donates body parts, an employment counselor, a professional softball player, a surgical nurse professional baseball player, and a daredevil who plays with dynamite among others. Through the monologues, each woman examines her life's work and explores the career that she has found. Or that has found her.